The Grunt

The Lonely Heart Series

Latrivia S. Nelson

RIVERHOUSE
PUBLISHING

www.riverhousepublishingllc.com

The Grunt

RiverHouse Publishing, LLC
5100 Poplar Avenue
Suite 2700
Memphis, TN 38117

All **RiverHouse, LLC** Titles, Imprints and Distributed Lines are available at special quantity discounts for bulk purchases for sales promotions, premiums, fund-raising and educational or institutional use.

First RiverHouse, LLC Trade Paperback Printing: 08/01/2011

1

ISBN: 978-0-9832186-8-5
ISBN: 0-9832-1868-5

Printed in the United States of America

This book is printed on acid-free paper.

www.riverhousepublishingllc.com

This book is dedicated to every man and woman who has ever served this country bravely. Thank you for your sacrifice and your courage. We are only safe to enjoy our liberty because of you.

A special thank you goes to my husband, Adam David Nelson, who served valiantly in the Marine Corp until he was wounded in Iraq then came home and faced a changed world courageously. He has been my best friend, a wonderful father, a kind husband and an outstanding provider.

I love you. I love you. I love you.

Acknowledgments

Kandace Tuggle, thanks for helping layout the cover for this book and all the others. I appreciate you and all that you do. Email her kandesigngrafix@gmail.com.

Adam Nelson, thanks for helping with the cover concept. We searched and searched until we found the perfect couple. The internet is amazing, isn't it?

Karen Moss, thanks for stepping up and helping me find a million errors in the book. As a devoted reader, service member and amazing woman, I truly admire your strength and courage. I'm happy to have you as my new eye. Trust me, I need it.

To the awesome staff at RiverHouse Publishing, thanks for your hard work and dedication to our dream of becoming a force in the industry. We may be small, but our hearts are big and mighty. No one ever achieved anything without first trying. Every day, we try and we succeed.

Thanks to every reader. The reason that I have gone from penning one book to ten is simply because of the amazing friendships that have flourished as a result. It is always a pleasure to write for you and to take you out of your normal day into the twisted, little mind of Latrivia S. Nelson.

Dear Reader,

The Lonely Heart Series is one my favorite projects, because it gives me an opportunity to focus on many types of relationships and all the ups and downs that come with them. Some of the stories are short like *The Ugly Girlfriend* and some of them are novel-length. However, each book has something special to share with you.

The Grunt is the third book in the series and probably one of the most personal. My husband is a Marine, as many readers know, and writing this story took me back to Camp Lejeune and all the wonderful and emotional moments as a Marine wife.

Brett and Courtney are a reflection of true love, letting your guard down, handling hard obstacles head on and having a little fun every once in awhile.

Now, there are some steamy love scenes in this book, but I wanted to show the passion between the characters and how being in stressful situations tend to work themselves out in the bedroom:-) There are also a few family fights, a few misunderstandings and plenty of drama. But it's all designed to give you a few hours of entertainment.

I hope that you enjoy my latest work, and I hope that you will continue to support me in the future.

God Bless & Much Happiness,

Latrivia S. Nelson

Chapter One

Camp Lejeune
Jacksonville, NC

The sun had already begun to set by the time Staff Sergeant Brett Black left the field. Throwing his gear in the back of his black Ford F-150, he pulled off his uniform cover and wiped his sweaty brow as he looked over the waterfront across from the company office.

Beautiful hues of gold splashed against the blue waters, and a tranquil breeze swept off the shore creating a picture-perfect evening. The view was something that should have calmed him, especially after a hectic day. Still, he had a bad feeling in his gut, like something eerie was on the horizon. And after three tours to Iraq and two tours to Afghanistan, he had learned that his gut was hardly ever wrong.

Running his large hand over his symmetric-al, dirty-blonde, high and tight haircut, he slipped on his Oakley shades and jumped in his truck. The smell of clean, hot leather greeted him, even burned him to the touch from being in the sun for over twelve hours.

Scanning the truck to make sure it was clean, a dirty little habit he had picked up in the Marine

Corps, he closed the door and slipped in his favorite Kong-Foo Fighters CD. It would be a long drive from the back of the base to the highway - plenty of time to clear his head before he got home. The music would help relax him, put him into a state of mind that would make him more pliable for home life, if you could call it that.

With the air blasting and the radio down, he headed out of Camp Lejeune, exhausted and starving, ready to get a shower and good night's sleep after seven long days of sleeping in tents and training on the rough terrain near highways and out in the bush. It would also be good to see his kid, and it might even be nice to see Amy, if she was in a good mood.

They had been on the outs since before Easter, and with Mother's Day approaching he wanted to get on his wife's good side for the holiday. She had been complaining more and more lately about him being away from home. In fact, it had been the conversation of their household for the last few months.

Brett rolled his eyes at the thought. Like he could help what the Marine Corps decided to do with him. It was almost laughable. If they said jump, the only reasonable question he could ask was how high. Still, Amy ragged him every chance she got about his absence in her life.

Their marriage was going south and his retirement with it, if he wasn't careful. They had been to two family counselors in the last year. Both were his idea, and neither had worked. Their last session had been cut short by Amy after she got extremely agitated. That day, she had taken the keys and left him in Jacksonville at the therapist's office, forcing him to call a ride to take him twenty-miles home to Swansboro.

Joe, his best friend and a fellow Marine, had picked him up that day and lectured him all the way home about getting his wife's growing antics under control. But such a thing was easier said than done.

Of course Amy had blamed it all on him, saying that he never seemed to realize how much damage him being gone all the time had done to their marriage.

Maybe she was right.

Still, he had to try.

Cameron was getting older, about to celebrate his fourth birthday in a few months, and he deserved to be raised in a two-parent household. The love for his son and the love he had for his wife had been the only two reasons that kept him from asking for a divorce himself. He still remembered the good times that they had back before she turned on him.

In fact, she had been the one who had suggested the Marine Corps when he was eighteen. It had been the only thing that he could recall that she had ever been so adamant about. Only after he was sworn in, everything went downhill. Amy was expecting some fairytale life but what she got was the reality of a military family – long days away, training, waiting and little pay.

Looking at his watch, he decided to pull into the grocery store and grab a little gift. Hopefully, roses could warm a spot in Amy's heart tonight and prevent another fight.

Pulling into a parking spot on the end of the first aisle, he jumped out and then looked down at his clothes. Shit. He couldn't go into a public establishment in his uniform. It was against the Uniform Code of Military Justice, and with his promotion pending, he was not going to get in trouble over something so trivial.

Jumping back inside his truck, he pulled up to the front of the grocery store and flagged down a teenage boy going inside.

"Hey, kid," Brett said, waving a twenty dollar bill.

Pulling at his saggy jeans, the teenager eyed the money and walked over to him. "You're in luck, dude. I only got one twenty-piece left," the boy said, digging in his front pocket.

Brett frowned. A twenty-piece? "No, I don't want any drugs," he said, flabbergasted. The boy couldn't have been a day over sixteen. And in the parking lot of the freaking grocery store? What was the world coming to? What the hell was he fighting for?

"Well then what'cha want?" the boy asked in his toughest voice.

"What do I want?" Leaning out of the truck, Brett flipped the boy's hat off his head, sending it to the ground, and growled. "I want you to take your little ass in there and get me a red bouquet of roses," he ordered. "You can keep the change. Consider it the only honest money that you've ever made in your little shitty life."

The teenager looked at the money for a minute then bent down and picked up his hat. "Get it yourself," he said, wiggling his freckled nose at Brett before he meandered off quickly with a bit of a dip in his step.

"Little prick!" Brett yelled. "If I didn't have to get home, I'd kick your little, drug-slinging ass!"

The boy looked back, evidently believing him, and quickly disappeared into the doors of the grocery store.

"Probably never worked an honest day in his little pathetic life," Brett said aloud as he put his truck in reverse. He'd have to forgo the roses tonight and hope that just his presence would be enough to make Amy happy, though he doubted it would be.

***

By the time that Brett got home, the sun had finally set. Pulling up to his lakeside cottage, he stopped to check the mail. The box was jam-packed as usual. It seemed that Amy hated checking the mail or doing any kind of chores. What seemed to confuse him more was why it was such a chore to check the mail, when she didn't have to pay one bill.

Flipping through the envelopes, he made his way up the drive to the porch and sat down on one of the white rocking chairs sitting in front of the bay windows.

Running his key under the flap of his cell phone bill, he pulled out the thick paper and turned to the last page. $400!

Gritting his teeth, he flipped through the pages to the itemized calls and saw that someone, not him, had been calling to Japan.

As the crickets chirped and the lightning bugs flew past him, he closed his eyes and tried to center himself. Taking a deep breath, he remembered that eerie feeling in his gut from earlier. It was right every single time.

Slapping a mosquito on his arm, he opened his eyes and looked at the bill again. Maybe there was a reasonable explanation, but he doubted it.

The only thing in Japan was other Marines and Sailors. And as far as he knew, none of his friends or their wives had been stationed there. So why was she calling to another country?

The creak of the front door made him move his gaze from the paper. Locking eyes on Amy as she leaned against the entryway, he tried to smile.

"Hey," he said in a deep baritone. He looked her up and down and watched her body language.

Relaxed, she gave a crooked smile. "Hey," she said in a deep southern drawl. "I didn't expect you home till tomorrow."

"I told you that I'd be home on Friday. It's Friday," he said, raising the cell phone bill in his hand. "Can we talk about this?" His brow rose.

Her gaze went from him to the paper then back to him. Frowning, she stood up straighter. "What about it?" Her voice was not as soft now.

"There are like three hundred dollars' worth of phone calls on your line to Japan," he said, standing up. He towered over her little body but his size didn't seem to bother her.

Smacking her lips, Amy turned and looked back in the house as Cameron started to cry.

"Momma's coming," she said to her son, closing the door without answering Brett.

Cursing under his breath, Brett caught the door before it could slam and followed after her. "Amy, who have you been calling?" he yelled out. He heard her feet as they stomped up the stairs. There was no way in hell he was going to let this go.

Sighing, he went back outside and grabbed his gear from the cab of the truck and threw his arms over the side. He didn't really have to ask. He knew who she'd been calling. A man. It didn't matter who, the point was that it was a man.

Looking back at the bricked house, illuminated by the open windows, he started to just get back in his truck and tear out of his cove, but he knew that he had to get an answer.

When he came back inside the house, Amy was in the kitchen throwing around plates. He could tell by the clink of the porcelain hitting the steel sink that she was on the war path.

After he dropped his sea bags in the laundry room, he quietly made his way into the kitchen and sat at the table. From behind, he could see her pouting. Slumped over under the fluorescent lights, she pursed her lips together and heaved out a frustrated breath from her nose.

"Who is it, Amy?" Brett asked, taking off his cover. His deep voice echoed throughout the kitchen.

"It's nobody," she bit out. "He's a friend."

"How do you know him?" He kept his eyes on her back.

"I met him at the gym. He's just a guy that I talk to sometimes."

"When did you meet him at the gym?"

Amy threw the plate down and turned around. "I don't know." She shrugged her thin shoulders. Her pebbled nipples showed through her thin, V-neck t-shirt. "About a year ago, when you were in Iraq. What's the big deal? He's just a friend that I talk to from time to time. He was transferred to Japan, and he doesn't have many friends over there. So, we talk."

Brett knew that she was lying. "Why would he make friends with a married woman? Why would you spend my money talking to him on the cell phone I bought you? What do you all have to talk about for hours?" He could feel the heat fuming under his collar. Seeing red, he looked down and realized that he was gripping the side of the table. Relaxing, he let go and waited for an answer to even one of his questions.

Amy watched him, unaffected by his mood. "What does it matter to you, Brett? You're never here."

"Here we go with this shit again! Dammit, Amy, don't I provide a decent life for you here? It's not like you have to work or do anything but take care of Cameron."

"Oh, like that's an easy job!" she snapped back.

"Are you seeing him?" he asked, breathing hard. "Are you seeing him?!!"

"He's in Japan. How in the hell could I be seeing him, Brett?" she asked, throwing down her washcloth. "You're never here. I never see you, and when you're here, you don't pay attention to me."

"That's not true," he said, lowering his voice. He shook his head. "What's his name?"

"So you can try to get him in trouble?" Amy snapped, rolling her eyes. "I wasn't born yesterday. You'll just look him up and call his command. Uh uh, that ain't happening."

Brett could feel himself losing control. Standing up from the table, he pushed the chair back and knocked it over. "Fine. I'll find out my damn self," he said, pulling the bill from the side pocket of his uniform pants.

"What are you doing?" she asked, walking up to him. She tried to snatch the bill from his hand, but he turned his back to block her.

Taking out his cell phone, he dialed the number all while absorbing the blows of Amy's small hands as she attacked him.

"Give me the damned phone, Brett!" she ordered as she started to cry.

Brett ignored her fake sobs for once and focused on his objective.

The phone rang several times before it went to voicemail. "Hi, you've reached Jermaine. Leave a message, and I'll hit you back as soon as I can. Peace."

Brett's face went blank. As soon as the phone beeped, he looked at Amy. "Jermaine, this is Brett Black, Amy Black's husband. When you get this message, give me a call back at 910-555-9313. I want to find out why the fuck you and my wife are having three-hour conversations." Hanging up the phone, he shook his head. "A black man?" He turned to her and gave an incredulous scowl.

"What are you, the grand dragon?" she asked him as she snatched the paper out of his hand and shoved it into her pocket.

Offended, Brett countered. "Hey, I'm not a racist. You know that. I just don't understand, considering that your redneck, Bible-thumping daddy may not be the grand dragon but he's definitely the second-in-charge. And you could easily be the fucking runner-up. I mean, with all the shit you gave me about being friends with Joe?"

She interrupted, putting her shaking finger up. "Jermaine is a friend. That's it. And I don't owe you no explanation." Pushing past him, she stomped out of the room and left him alone in the kitchen.

Brett was speechless. He stood by the table in a daze and listened to her stalk up the stairs and violently slam their bedroom door behind her.

"Son of bitch," he said aloud. He knew without a doubt that Jermaine was no friend, and he was no idiot. Still, to run upstairs and stir up more trouble would only make him look like a fool, and he felt foolish enough for the minute.

Amy had never been culturally sensitive. In fact, she was always making snide remarks about Black people, Latinos and whoever else happened to be on her bad side. So, the fact that she was calling Japan to talk to a Black man floored him. How could a woman who was so opposed to everyone who wasn't wearing a cowboy hat and flying a confederate flag suddenly confiding in a Black man? And how had he not noticed?

Nothing fit anymore.

Questions assailed him like bullets in a firefight. Wasn't he supposed to get some credit for providing her a lifestyle that never included work or worry while he, conversely, worked himself to the bone?

What had this guy ever done for her? Had Jermaine paid their bills? Had Jermaine sat up at night after working all day with their son when he was teething, sick or scared? Had Jermaine spent his off days cleaning their gutters, cutting their yard, trying to save their marriage? Now suddenly, he was the bad guy?

Unbelievable!

Overwhelmed, Brett screamed out suddenly and hit the wall, knocking the magnetic clipboard to the floor. His fist left a hole in the drywall. Pulling his hand out, sore and red from the impact, he leaned against the door and shook his head. Why do I even try anymore? he asked himself.

Cameron, his three-year-old son, walked in-to the kitchen and tugged on his leg, all but ignoring his father's fit. Brett looked down at the little guy and tried to smile. It was comical but he tried.

Running a hand through his son's tousled brown locks, he picked him up and kissed his rosy cheeks. "Where have you been?" Brett asked, holding him in his arms as he walked over to the refrigerator to find something to eat. Kids didn't like ruckus. He knew that, even if he didn't know anything else anymore. It was best that he control his anger for his son's sake.

That was another thing. Was it too much to ask to get a hot meal in his own home? Hell, he'd settle for takeout. He just wanted a little effort. He wanted more than his wife spending half her day on Facebook or curled up surfing the Internet on her laptop, ignoring him when he was at home and giving him dirty looks every time that he said a word to her about it.

"Are you and Mommy fighting again?" Cameron asked in a raspy voice, pulling Brett out of his thoughts.

"No," Brett lied, pulling out a seasoned steak wrapped in plastic. "Are you hungry?"

"Yes. I want cereal," the boy said, running his small hand over his father's five o'clock shadow.

"It's too late for cereal. Do you want me to fix you a steak?" Brett asked, setting him on the floor.

"I don't want steak, Daddy. I want cereal," Cameron protested.

Brett didn't really feel like arguing with his son, too. Amy had taken the cake for the day. Although, his mom would have had a heart attack if she were not already dead over him fixing breakfast food so late in the evening.

Going to the cupboard, he pulled out a small blue bowl and went into the pantry to grab

Cameron's favorite frosted flakes. "How are you ever going to get big like daddy, if you don't eat any protein?" Brett asked, pouring the cereal reluctantly.

"What's protein?" Cameron asked, pulling his plastic solider toys from his pocket. The boy was never without a toy.

"Never mind. I'll explain it to you later," Brett said, putting Cameron's bowl on the table. "Eat up, little guy."

Grabbing a beer from the refrigerator, he walked upstairs past the toys lining the steps and tried to open his bedroom door. "Open up, Amy," he ordered, leaning his head against the wall. His hand lingered on the knob.

"Leave me alone!" she screamed out. "Sleep on the fucking couch!"

He could hear her shuffling around in the room. Twisting the knob again, he protested. "We need to talk. This isn't just going to go away." His voice cracked. All the fight was nearly gone in him, but he still wanted to try to come to some type of understanding.

"There is nothing to talk about," she said with a sniffle in her quivering, little voice.

Brett felt hopeless and exhausted. If he persisted, she would simply shut him out more. They would probably spend the entire rest of the night arguing if she did open the door, and he didn't want that either. Plus, he was starting to get a headache. He felt it every time he turned his head, pounding in his temples like hot pokers.

Letting go of the door, he took a big gulp of his beer, looked at the door one last time and headed back down the stairs quietly. He'd discuss this with her tomorrow. For now, he just needed to eat and get some rest.

Chapter Two

The sun beamed into the den through the white, faux-wooden plantation blinds right into Brett's eyes while he slept. Turning his face from the window, he pulled the thin sheet over himself and tried to ignore the coming day.

Having slept all night on the sofa, he felt his body kinked up and begging to stretch out, but he tried to ignore that too and get a few more minutes of shut eye. God knew that he needed it. He had stayed up for hours the night before mulling over his situation, and no matter how he approached it, it still looked bleak.

It would have been better for him to have just slept on the floor last night, but after a week on the ground while out in the field, he wanted to lay horizontal on something elevated - anything would do. Hell, he would have slept on the kitchen table last night if he had to.

With his arm thrown up over his face, he felt himself start to ease back into a light sleep when the television turned on suddenly. SpongeBob blasted through the surround sound jolting him out of any comfort that he had found.

"Cameron," he growled, sitting up. Blinking heavy-lidded eyes, he pushed his body to the back of the leather sofa. "Can't you go and watch

TV somewhere else, man? Daddy really wants to try to sleep for a little while longer." His voice lightened when he made eye contact with his son. None of this was his fault. Yet, he was the one being ignored.

Still in his pajamas, Cameron walked over to his daddy with the remote in hand and sat in his lap. "Mommy's gone," the boy said flatly.

Brett wiped his eyes again. "She probably went to the store or to the gym," he assured Cameron.

Reaching over to the end table, he picked up his watch and looked at the time. 7:15 a.m. Deciding that trying to sleep any later was completely futile, he moved his son beside him and amped himself up. It was time to face the day, time to go and get in Amy's ass. Now that he had gotten a little sleep, he would be quicker with his responses, more apt to dig into this Jermaine thing without giving in.

"Mommy's gone away," Cameron said, more solemn. He dropped the remote and looked up at his daddy.

With his elbows planted on his knees, Brett heaved a tired sigh into his hands and smelled his own breath. Horrid. "I'm sure that she'll be back."

"She took all of her clothes," Cameron explained.

Brett paused and went stiff as a board. Looking straight ahead at the television, he swallowed hard. His deep baritone lowered. "Where did she take her clothes?" He turned to his son and waited for an answer.

"She put them in her car," Cameron answered, dangling his feet off the side of the couch. "Is she coming back, daddy? Did she move?"

In only his black boxer shorts, Brett jumped up and headed out the room. His dog tags jingled on his chiseled, tan chest as he moved. Stopping as he got to the door, he looked back at his son. "Stay right here and watch TV, okay." He tried to take the worry out of his voice, but he had that eerie feeling in his gut again.

Cameron nodded obediently and then turned towards the television.

Closing the door behind him, Brett ran as quietly as he could through the hall, up the back-stairs to their bedroom. Pushing the door open with his index finger, he looked inside.

"Amy?" he called out, walking into the room slowly. There was no answer. "Amy, are you in here?" he called again. His bare feet stuck to something on the hardwood floor. He raised his foot to see that it was gum.

With the wind blowing through the open windows cloaked in white linen curtains, the tranquility of the large bedroom was strangely deceiving. The airy space appeared to be undisturbed except for pictures of Cameron on the nightstand that were now gone. She had left their wedding photos on the bed but had taken the expensive frames that his mother had given them. He gazed down at the photos and shook his head in disbelief. She had always been a tacky bitch.

Going to their white wooden dresser, he pulled open the top drawer and discovered that all of her things were missing. He stared at the empty drawer blankly. In disbelief, he opened the small jewelry box on top of the dresser where they kept a small roll of cash and saw that it too was gone, along with all of her jewelry.

Now, he was getting pissed.

Dashing to the closet, he pulled open the door and saw that all of her dresses, pants, skirts, belts and shoes were gone. The same for her backpack that housed her laptop, I-pod and camera – the essentials of her small-minded life. Everything that belonged to Amy Black was gone and so was she.

Sitting on the bed, he ran his shaking hand over his face and closed his eyes. His heart raced so loud until it pounded into his ears. He could feel his hands clamming with nervousness. The room seemed to be closing in on him one thought at a time. Shuddering apart inside, he tried to get his baring. He just couldn't believe his eyes. She was gone. Just like that. No warning. No signs. Or like everything else, maybe he simply hadn't noticed.

Taking a deep breath, he reached over to the night stand and grabbed the house phone. He dialed her cell phone number hoping that she'd answer. A computer message answered instead. It had been disconnected. Slowly putting down the phone, he let out a defeated sigh. What was he going to do now?

Cameron stuck his head into the door with a curious smile. Like everyone else in the house, he hadn't listened to Brett. "Is Mommy coming back, Daddy?" he asked, standing in the door with his teddy bear in his small, pudgy hand. His worried eyes met his father's, hoping for comfort, sensing that something was wrong.

Brett knew that this was a defining moment in a father's life.

"Come here," Brett said, reaching out his hands.

Cameron walked over to him and put his arms out. Brett picked him up and nuzzled his nose into his son's hair as he replayed the night before in his mind. Amy wouldn't have been stupid enough to charge all those calls on her phone unless she had a plan. This had not been a spur-of-the-moment decision.   She had planned to leave them alone.

Thinking back, he did recall the month before when she was frantically searching for her passport. At the time, it didn't make any sense to him, but now he understood the urgency. There was no way to get to Japan without it. Only, he didn't understand what she was going to do when she got there.   Marines couldn't live off base because of safety issues and there was no way that the Corps was going to let her stay with him. Maybe Jermaine was just one stop of her quest to get as far away from him as possible.

Looking at his son, he held back his anger and tried to give the young boy a smile. He didn't see the purpose of telling such a small child that his mother had just abandoned him. What he did need to do, however, was find out what legal steps he needed to take to protect himself and Cameron.   The gloves were officially off.   He would have to stomp her into the ground, figuratively speaking. However, if she had been a man, he would have already kicked her back-stabbing ass all over the Pacific Rim.

Picking his son up, he turned off the light and closed the door to the room without looking back. There was nothing but bad memories in there. Just like any other problem in the Marine Corps, the only thing that he could do was prepare a counterstrike, since he had already been attacked. Amy Black had all but tried to sever his balls.

Taking his son to his bathroom, he turned on the water to the tub and dropped in the yellow rubber ducky and boat on the shelf. "Let's get you cleaned up so that we can head into town," Brett said, grabbing the SpongeBob bubble bath. For the moment, things still were quite surreal. He moved around mindlessly.

"Where are we going, Daddy?" Cameron asked, pulling off his dingy Spiderman pajamas.

"To the library," Brett answered, trying to push Amy out of his mind for the moment.

"Why are we going there?" Cameron asked as he stuck his little fingers in the tub to wade in the water.

Brett sighed and grabbed a large towel from the shelf. "Daddy needs to get a few books," he said, omitting that he needed to find out how to file for divorce in the state of North Carolina. With the JAG office closed until Monday, he would have to use the resources available to him until he could get back on base and find out what his rights were.

***

After a quick stop at Burger King for a kids' meal for Cameron, it occurred to Brett that in all of the hysteria, he had not checked his banking account.   As soon as the thought crossed his mind, he felt another pang in his gut, but he was too afraid to call the 800 number and find out if his suspicions were correct. A man couldn't take that kind of news behind the wheel.

Speeding out onto the highway, he zipped past the library and headed straight to Jacksonville.

When he got to his bank on the outskirts of town, he barely missed them closing up for the day. With Cameron in-hand, he yanked off his shades as he entered the building and sat down with the first customer service representative who would see him.

"How can I help you today, Mr. Black?" a slender Asian man asked, offering a seat across from his desk.

"I need to take my wife off of my account and find out how much money I have in the bank," Brett said, sitting Cameron in the chair beside him.

After giving his access number and showing the man his bank card and ID, the customer service rep typed in something to his computer and paused. Looking hesitantly over at Brett then Cameron, he pulled his monitor where Brett could see.

"There was a transfer this morning to another account by Mrs. Black in the amount of $40,000.

You currently have a balance of $10,000 in your savings account and $3,500 in your checking," he said, lowering his voice. "And I'm sorry, but since this is a joint account, you can't take her name off the account without her permission. She'll have to come in with you." The man braced for the explosion. Having worked near a military base for over five years, he had seen all manner of broken relationships and clearly identified this as one of them.

The color left Brett's face. "What!?" he exclaimed, nearly jumping out of his seat. "That's half of our life savings. What the fuck? How can she do that?" he asked, exasperated. He leaned over on the desk and put his hands on his head. He had never hyperventilated before, but he could tell that he was close. Bombs and bullet he could handle. Having half of his money snatched from under him was a completely different ball game.

Other customers looked over at him as he experienced a total melt down. They whispered and watched in amusement.

"I'm so sorry, Mr. Black. The best thing that I can suggest is to open another account and transfer what is left of your money to that account in your name only." He paused to make sure that Brett was getting all of this.

Brett looked over at his son and gritted his teeth. "I just signed up for another four years with the fucking Corps. She took half of my bonus, left me with my kid and you're telling me that there is nothing that I can do?"

"I'm sorry, sir. By law, there is nothing that we can do," the Asian man said sympathetically. "You may want to see if there is some way you can go through your chain of command to seek additional assistance."

Brett sat back in the chair and laughed. His large hand ran over his mouth, holding back a string of curse words. Looking around at the attention that he had drawn to himself, he swallowed down the news and threw up his hands. "Just... get me a new account for now, before my son and I are in a homeless shelter," he said, breathing out a frustrated sigh through his flaring nostrils.

"Right away, sir. Can I offer you something to drink?"

"You got some whiskey back there?" Brett asked, rolling his eyes.

***

The Swansboro Library was bustling with people. On a Saturday in a small town, however, there wasn't much else to do but go to the beach, go shopping or dining or go the library. Parking towards the back of the yellow-bricked building,

Brett unbuckled Cameron from his baby seat and made his way inside. He walked in a daze, numb from the day's events. He had felt less anxiety in Iraq during a full-on firefight than right now. Yet, he had to keep it together for his son, who so far had remained calm throughout their debacle.

The relentless hot sunrays beat down on the pair as they walked. Cameron fidgeted, tugging at his pull-up and begging his father to pick him up, while Brett pulled him along and wiped at his sweaty brow. The perspiration at his collar left a wet ring around his blue polo and made his clothes stick to his skin. It was all the makings for a complete melt down, yet he tried with all his might to hold on.

As they entered the air-conditioned building, the cool air calmed their senses. A few women in the corner, who were reading to their children, locked their eyes on Brett and Cameron, admiring the attractive doting father and his charming son who on the outside seemed to be part of a picture perfect family. If they only knew, he thought to himself.

Brett skimmed the small space, looking for the reference room and a possible answer to his ramping problems. Normally, he would have gone on the Internet at home and found the information he needed, but Amy had taken their only computer with her.

He spotted the reference section and headed directly to it. Picking Cameron up to move faster, he strode through the happy families to the quiet empty room and stepped inside. The small space was stacked with books, too many to decipher which one he needed. Rusty on his dewy decimal skills, he stood in the middle of the room like a lost child.

"Why can't I just catch a break," he said, immediately berating himself for showing even a glimpse of self-pity.

"You look a little loss," a soft voice said from behind Brett.

Turning around, Brett locked his eyes on a dark-skinned black woman, holding a handful of books in her arms.

Quickly, he boxed all of his drama up. "I'm looking for books on...divorce," he said in a deep baritone, looking down at Cameron. He knew that Cameron had no idea what the word meant, still he was leery of using it in front of him for fear that he might repeat it.

"Oh," the woman said, walking past him over to the corner of the room. Her perfume wafted up to his nose. "You need to look over here," she said, placing her pile of books on the table in front of the bookshelf.

Tied in a pink bow, her long ebony hair was pulled off her deep brown face in a delicate ponytail. In a pink button down, starched and tucked in perfectly to dark jeans that fit her wide hips and short legs, she seemed overtly gentle and feminine to him. And it wasn't that he was trying to notice her; it was simply that her presence commanded it, even in his current chaotic state.

With hazel-colored eyes, she turned and peaked back at him with a gentle smile that showed the deep dimples in her oval face as she flipped through the books. Her manicured nails caressed the books gracefully as she turned back to pull a few from the shelf. "I'm not sure which ones you need, but these should help."

Brett watched her every graceful movement. She regarded the books like she was the mistress of literature, pursing her lip as she thoughtfully pulled each one from the sea of hardbacks in front of her.

Pulling out a black, leather-bound book, she reached out and passed them to him, brushing his hand as she did so. The touch made him feel uncomfortable, like he had touched something sacred, something he had no right to feel.

The woman looked down at Cameron with raised brows, interested in the rosy-cheeked boy. Bending down, she ran her hand over Cameron's curly brown locks. Her gentle voice was like silk against Brett's ears. "You know, we're having reading time right now over in the center. Why don't I take you over and introduce you to the other kids, while your father looks for what he needs." She looked back up at Brett for his approval.

Brett would normally not trust anyone with his son, but the lady seemed warm and nurturing, unlike his blood-sucking wife. Plus, he needed a minute alone to gather his thoughts, box up his frustrations and make a plan that didn't involve a shot gun and a k-bar.

"That would be great. Thanks," Brett said, clearing his throat. His face suddenly warmed, showing his gratitude through the sudden rush of color to his peaked features.

She nodded at him and took Cameron's hand. As she passed quietly, he caught another whiff of her perfume. It smelled of roses, like the ones he wanted to buy Amy the night before. The thought made his stomach cramp.

Left alone for the moment, he took the book and sat down at the table with his pen and note-pad. The room smelled like books. Ink, a bit of dust and supreme knowledge radiated through the small place as the sun beamed in through the elevated windows.

"Do you need anything else?" the woman asked, walking back into the room to collect the books that she had left after she had squared away Cameron.

Brett looked up at her. "No, ma'am," he said, hitting his pen on the table. "Are there more books on divorce out there?" For a moment, he was able to take his focus off of Amy, distracted by her striking beauty.

The woman paused, looking deep into his blue eyes. "Everything you need is in this room," she said, piling the books in her embrace again.

If only that were true, he thought to himself. Brett smirked at her statement then tucked in his chin and focused on the book in front of him.

"I'm Courtney by the way," she said as she got to the threshold of the door. "Just in case you need anything."

Brett looked up at her and nodded. "I'm Brett," he said with a smile. He couldn't believe that he could even muster such a thing in the state that he was in, but she sort of pulled it out of him. The idea stalled him. Maybe there was life after Amy.

As if reading his mind, she smiled. The innocent gesture was so provocative to him that he was forced to turn to face her. "Nice to meet you, Brett," Courtney said, shifting her weight from one foot to the other. "Your son is in the play center. I'll keep an eye on him until you're done."

"Thanks," Brett said, trying not to blatantly stare at her. "I shouldn't be too long. I don't even know what I'm looking for."

"Seek and ye shall find," she whispered as she closed the door.

He quickly turned his head back to the book. Why couldn't he have run into a woman like that instead of a man-eater?

An hour turned to three hours, and before Brett knew it, the library was closing. With Cameron sitting across from him drawing on a piece of paper, he stapled his notes together and yawned. He had a few options in front of him, first to file abandonment, and secondly to notify his chain-of-command. In court, she wouldn't stand a chance, but he still had to figure out what to do about his son.

He had never handled childcare before. Normally, Amy stayed at home with Cameron unless she sent him to Mom's Day Out at the local church. Now, he had to figure out if he could get Cameron onto a list for emergency care. Unfortunately to do so, he would have to get the Marine Corps involved in his marriage. That was typically a no-no. No one discussed home and never let it affect the job. In fact, the guys who did have to have the Marine Corps help manage their families would often be looked down upon, but how much further down could he go?

He was clueless about where to begin. Amy had also been kind enough to leave a small note in the downstairs bathroom explaining that things were not working out for her with him and that she needed to move on with her life. And since Cameron was a young man, Brett could raise him better than she could. And that was it. No mention of love or sorrow just that she had to move on like their marriage had meant less than nothing. After that, he knew that there was no need to do any more looking for Amy. She had skipped town, and he was now a single father.

The problem that he currently faced was that he was an active-duty grunt in the Marine Corps. He spent more days in the field training than he did at home. Outside of filing for a hard-ship and risking his career, the only thing that he could do was find a babysitter and develop a plan for childcare. He had risked his life for his country, given up everything including some personal rights to be called a Marine, and there was no way in hell he was going to watch it all be flushed down the drain by anyone.

Courtney waited until all the other patron's had left and it was time to set the alarm before she bothered them. Walking into the room, she waved at Cameron and slid Brett a Styrofoam cup of coffee. Nodding, she hunched her thin shoulders. "You look like you could use it," she said, noting the tiredness in his eyes.

"I normally don't do coffee," he said, picking the cup up, "but maybe this will do something for me that the water isn't doing." Putting the cup to his lips, he took a sip and sighed. It did feel good going down.

"It will make you more alert," she said, looking over at Cameron. "And it will make him less of a handful."

Brett nodded in agreement. "Do you have kids?"

"No," she said, shaking her head. "I work around them all day." Biting her lip, she looked at her watch. "I hate to put you boys out, but we're closing up for today."

"Oh, sorry," Brett said, pushing away from the table.

"I'll give you a minute to get things together."

"Thanks," he said, taking another sip of coffee, "for everything."

"No problem. Just turn off the light and close the door when you get all of your papers together, and I'll be waiting right outside here."

"I'll only be a minute," he said, gathering all of his papers quickly.

"Okay, but take your time and make sure you don't forget anything. We're closed on Sundays," Courtney said, quietly exiting the room.

Brett covertly watched her hips as she turned and left them. That was wrong of him to do, especially in his situation, still he snuck a look. Being around such a soft-spoken woman who showed the least bit of concern for him was a breath of fresh air. It roused his primal senses involuntarily and reminded him of what a shitty hand he had been dealt.

"Are you hungry again, man?" Brett asked, stretching and taking his mind off of both Amy and the librarian.

"Can we have Burger King?" Cameron asked, wide-eyed.

"You just had Burger King for lunch," Brett reminded. "How about I go home and fix us something to eat?"

"Please, Daddy. I want Burger King," Cameron pleaded.

Brett gave in. "Fine. Burger King it is." At least he wasn't asking for cereal.

***

The music blasted in Brett's truck as he pulled into his cove. Cameron had finally fallen asleep in the back with his Sippy cup pressed firmly to his pouty lips, exhausted from their tour de Swansboro. And Brett had finally calmed down and come to some realization of what had happened to him in the last six hours. That was until he noticed two vehicles in his driveway.

"What the hell is it now?" he asked aloud as he pulled up to his house.

He wasn't sure if he could take anything else.

Stepping out of his truck and leaving Cameron safely inside, he saw First Sergeant Newman, a chaplain and a silver-haired man in a black suit waiting for him. Evidently, news had traveled fast to the base about his sudden fate, but he couldn't understand how they knew already unless Amy had told them.

First Sergeant Newman was the first to approach. Wearing his desert uniform and a frown, he approached, extending his large hand to Brett.

"How are you, Brett," he said with worry in his voice.

It was highly unusual for his superior to address him so informally. Shaking his hand, Brett looked around at his small audience concerned. "Had a long day, First Sergeant and it isn't getting any shorter," he said, clenching his keys in his other hand.

"This is Chaplain Myers. I believe that you all met when Lance Corporal Williams died," the First Sergeant said, stepping to the side to allow Chaplain Myers to shake Brett's hand as well.

"Yeah, how are you, sir?" Brett asked confused. Since when did the military send out a chap-lain for a divorce?

"Nice to meet you, Staff Sergeant Black," Chaplain Myers said in a warm voice. His smile suggested that someone had died. Considering his mother had recently passed in the last year and he was the only child, nothing made sense.

"What's going on?" Brett asked, looking over at the unidentified man, standing a few feet away. "Who's the civilian?"

They all looked back at the man.

"That's Kevin Daugherty. He's with Southern Atlantic Airlines. He needs to talk to you," First Sergeant said, moving closer to Brett. "It's best that we step inside."

"Why? What's going on?" Brett asked alarmed.

"It's about your wife," Chaplain Myers answered. "Have you seen the news at all this morning?"

"No," Brett answered as his eyes darted back to his truck. "I've been sort of busy."

"Well, that is why we're here. Why don't we step inside?" Myers suggested again, motioning towards Brett's front door.

"No," Brett answered defensively. "What's going on?" he demanded.

First Sergeant took a deep breath and put his hand on his hip. "Amy's plane never made it to her destination, Brett. It went down a couple of hours ago. We couldn't reach you on your cell. Your wife is dead."

Chapter Three

Brett's best friend, Joe, came over as soon as Brett called him. Hauling his wife, Judy, with him, he dashed from Jacksonville in their Dodge mini-van packed with kids straight from Wal-Mart to the small township of Swansboro with the blinkers flashing.

When they arrived, Brett was sitting on the porch steps in a daze, staring out in blankness with papers clutched in his hand. Sweat poured down his face and soaked his shirt; his skin had started to burn, reddening around his forehead and cheeks. Yet, he sat baking in the sun like he didn't feel it.

Brett barely acknowledged his friends as they approached. He even ignored the children as they crawled all over him to get into the house with Cameron. With a little more care, Judy bypassed quietly, moving past him on the steps to follow the children. But Joe came and sat beside him on the step, slowly easing the paper out of his friend's hand to read the news in print.

It had taken a moment to get Brett to stand up and go into the house. But Joe knew the right words to say to snap his friend out of it. And it had taken even longer to get him to speak. But

Joe was good at that too, and in his own little way he coerced him out of his shell.

Slowly, Brett moved back into reality, though it wasn't easy to be there at the moment. He had seen many things, very gruesome things, and he had held it together through all of it. But never in his life did he expect to be burying what was left of his wife at such a young age, nor did he expect the things that happened preceding her death. It was all a dreamlike experience that seemed to get worse as the day went on. He was almost afraid to see what would happen next. Yet, finally, the eerie feeling in his stomach had sub-sided. He hoped that meant the hysteria was over.

While the kids played in the backyard, Brett sat at the kitchen table looking through the paper-work that Mr. Daugherty had left regarding his rights. Supposedly, in a freak malfunction, the plane that was to take his wife from Jacksonville to her lover in Japan had suddenly gone down taking all of its passengers with it about an hour after takeoff and crashed into a patch of farm land. There were no survivors. Not one. He dwelled on that fact for a while after he heard it, thinking that just because Amy deserved to be burned to a stake didn't mean that everyone else should have. He wasn't sure if he was sadder about her death or the strangers that he had never met.

He had decided as soon as he heard the news to keep the fact that his wife was leaving him to himself. Instead, he had stood in a stupor, trying to process everything that had suddenly happened. He had just gone from a husband to part of an abandoned family to a widower in half a day. Talk about a blink of an eye. His life seemed to be moving at warp speed.

The only people who did know the truth about his tragedy were sitting across from him at the table looking nearly as shocked as he was.

"The Marine Corps is going to give me a few days to get all the arrangements together. They have a liaison who's going to help me get some emergency care for Cameron, and the chaplain is suggesting counseling, which the airline will pay for," Brett said, looking up from the paper.

"I hope that they plan to pay for a hell of a lot more than that," Joe said absently.

"I'm sure that they will," Brett said, sipping his beer.

"I hate to ask, but did you have a life insurance policy?" Judy asked, looking over at Joe for approval of her input.

Brett nodded. "Yeah, the same as we all have. $100,000 payable immediately according to First Sergeant."

"Well, at least that will cover the money she took," Joe said, immediately wishing he could take back his words. "Shit, man, I didn't mean it that way." He did. He just didn't expect the truth to come out so bluntly.

Brett raised his trembling hand. "It's okay. I know." He shook his head. "I just can't believe that she's gone. I mean, it was hard enough to know that she was gone...leaving me, but to know that she's now dead..." His words trailed off as he zoned out again. He almost laughed at the satire.

Judy stood up and picked up their plates. She had fixed them an afternoon meal from the groceries that they had just purchased before coming over. Going to the sink, she immediately began to clean.

Joe could look at his friend and tell that he needed a man minute. Standing up, he motioned towards the door. "How about we go and get some fresh air," he said to Brett.

Standing up, Brett followed him outside to the front porch. Everything seemed bizarre to him at the moment, every movement, every room, every person. It was there, but it wasn't. With shallow breaths, he tried his hardest to hold on to his fleeting reality.

"Do you want us to take Cameron for a day or two?" Joe asked as he dug a pack of cigarettes out of his front pocket. Pulling out a single Kool, he offered one to Brett.

"You know I just quit a freaking month ago," Brett said, taking the cigarette from Joe. Lighting the end of the cigarette as he held it in between his full lips, he took a drag and squinted up into the setting sun.

Joe watched his friend for a moment and lit his own. Leaning against the white wooden railing, he stared off. They had been boys for four years. They had served in Iraq and had gone through the perils of married life together. Still, he often marveled at their friendship and their closeness, considering when he had first met Brett, he thought him to be another close-minded redneck.

However, Brett had proven Joe wrong. He had a very open, liberal mind about most things and didn't make a difference between his black and white Marines. He had never given him shit in the past about being one of the only black men in Bravo Company Recon unit or the fact that he was married to a white woman. He had never asked his view point about President Obama, assuming that just because he was black that he had to be a democrat, which he was. But that was beside the point. He had never treated his bi-racial children any different from Cameron. In fact, Brett had never mentioned race at all to him. The only thing he did discuss in length was his rocky marriage to Amy.

No one had approved of her. Sure, she was easy on the eyes – a fair, thin woman barely 100 pounds and fighting for every inch that made her a solid five feet tall. Her big blue eyes and bleached blonde hair matched her saline breasts and French-manicured nails. Amy Black had been the talk of the base. She always worked out during the lunch hour, catching the eye of many higher ups in the grunt gym that she faithfully frequented. And on several occasions, while none of the accusations had been founded, she had been linked to a couple of officers in the town bar.

No, no one had approved of her with her Southern charm and her short skirts, her incessant demands of Brett and her drama queen antics that had landed him in a few uncomfortable situations that caused him to move off the base and out of free housing into their current home - a place she had to have because she just couldn't take being around other Marine wives.

Joe thought that Amy wanted to move out to Swansboro to have more privacy in order to do her dirt without anyone finding out. He believed the stories of her one-night stands with anything with rank and her desire to move up the Marine Corps ladder from being a Sergeant's wife to being an officer's wife with a blue sticker on the front of her blue Ford Focus instead of the red one she had reluctantly been forced to brandish.

Every opportunity she could get, she stressed to Brett the need for him to go to college and get a degree so that he could go to Officer Candidate School, never taking into consideration that while he was determined to be a lifer in the Marine Corps, he was also happy to be an enlisted man. It was her pressure on him that caused his relentless drive, even when he was already one of the best Marines in the fleet and her demands of him that caused his continued unhappiness with himself.

Joe was actually happy that she was gone, and while he hated that she had to go down in flames literally, he felt that she had gotten what was coming to her.

Brett finally snapped out of his daze and realized that they had been standing in silence for a while. Going back to the question that Joe had asked, he flipped the butt of his cigarette over the rail into the bushes and sighed. "Cameron should stay here with me. I'll be alright. In fact, he might help me get through this." He said so with hope.

"You sure?" Joe asked. "You have a lot to do. You have to plan a funeral with her family, get him into some kind of child care, see a counselor, get a lawyer to sue the pants off this airline and still be ready to rock and roll with the Corps."

The list sounded daunting to Brett, but he pushed out his chest and rose to the occasion. "As long as I can call you guys if I need to, I think that I'll be fine."

"Well, you know you can call us. Judy only works part-time at the Naval Hospital. She'd love to help you watch Cameron."

"Now that I've got some extra money, I think that I'll try to get someone to come into the house and stay with him...just until I get up on my feet."

Joe had nearly forgotten about the insurance money. Nodding, he thumped his cigarette. "Sounds good. Why don't we leave Judy to do her thing? She's going to be in there cleaning for a minute. And the kids are having fun in the back. You and I could go out to the beach. I think Anderson's having a cookout tonight."

"Sounds like a plan," Brett said, fishing out his keys. "I could use something stronger than a beer right now, anyway."

***

Emerald Isle was only a few minutes away from Swansboro, but it seemed as though Brett was driving into another world. He went from the quiet, tranquil middle-class community by the lake where his home was to the playground for retired officers and business moguls by the Oceanside.

The upscale homes that lined the waterway were all complimented by extravagant boats docked at their backdoors and luxury cars parked in their multi-car garages.

Palm trees swayed in the night air and sparkling stars and a full moon shone down on his black truck as he let his elbow rest on his open window. He looked around and shook his head. This is the life, he thought to himself.

Brett knew that he had no bright ambitions that would land him as a resident in Emerald Isle, and he had no desire to be anything other than what he was. Yet, when he drove over from his world to this one, he always felt a sense of wonder. What were the people who lived here like? How did the other half live? Did they have the same type of worries that he did? Did their wives leave in the middle of the night? Did they know what it was like to sign their lives over for another four years of possible death just to have sense of security for the moment? The world will never know, he thought to himself.

With a cigarette hanging out of his mouth and Kung-Foo Fighters playing on his radio, he watched the sun trail behind him as he drove over the bridge to his friend's waterfront condo to let his hair down for a minute. He could feel

Joe look over at him every once in a while to see
if he had finally broken, to see if he had cracked.
Yet, strangely enough, Brett still felt numb, which
allowed him to hold it together.

"I'm fine," Brett finally said, releasing smoke
from his mouth.

"You sure?" Joe asked, turning down the radio.

Brett looked down at Joe's hand. Didn't he
know that a man should never touch another
man's radio? Rush Hour 2 flashed through his
mind and he cracked a smile.

Joe was confused by Brett's sudden smile.
Frowning, he sat back in his chair and put his
elbow on the window. "Want to talk about it?"

Brett drove quietly, every once in a while
checking his rearview mirror. "She didn't love
me," he said flatly. "She was leaving me, and had
it not been for the plane crash, she would have
been in another man's arms by tomorrow. How
am I supposed to feel about that?" He looked
over at Joe for an answer.

"You're supposed to feel as betrayed as you
obviously do feel. I know what hurts more is that
she left Cameron."

"Makes me wonder if she loved either one of
us," Brett concluded.

"Young women are hard to read. That is why I
love Judy. She's pretty dependable. She might
not be a size two, but her heart is made of pure 14

carat gold." Joe smiled at the thought of her, but he quickly remembered that his friend was mourning and reigned in his own joy. "What you need to focus on now is a plan."

"You know what really ticks me off?" Brett said, going back to Amy. "And I don't mean this in a racial way... she was leaving me for a black man. You knew Amy. She was by all accounts a racist."

"Yeah, she was a redneck," Joe said absently. He looked out the window.

Brett laughed. "Exactly." He wiped his nose. "It just goes to show that I didn't know that woman one damn bit."

Joe smacked his lips. "Well, you can't beat yourself up over it. You didn't do anything wrong. Everything that happened came about because of her decisions. Karma's just a bitch like that."

Brett shook his head in agreement. Karma was a bitch, but at least for now it was in his favor.

***

Anderson's place was packed at dusk. Marines and women crowded the small two-bedroom condo and spilled out onto the deck and beach. Music blasted on the stereo and the television played the New York Yankee's baseball game. People hooked up on the couches and in the bathroom, while some just rolled around on the floor. It was by all accounts a party. Girls. Beer. Lots of making out. And no regrets. A perfect place for Brett.

While some of the men gathered at the grill to pass off food to those waiting, Brett stood talking to Anderson in the small kitchenette.

Quietly, he had told his good friend about his misfortune and received the almost exact response. Apathy. No one liked Amy. And no one was sad to see her go. They did not even pretend, which made it further possible for Brett to come to terms with his feelings.

Terry Anderson was a Staff Sergeant in Recon as well. Divorced twice and one kid, the clean-cut surfer spent most of his time chasing skirts or riding waves when he wasn't at the base. And he had developed quite a reputation on base and in all the surrounding cities for being a womanizer. However, he and Brett were close- nearly as close and Brett and Joe – because of the time that they had spent in Iraq together.

With his hand up against the vent of his stove, Anderson cooked baked beans and watched the young women as they passed by, sizing each one up for later. He finally looked over at Brett and shook his head. "Man that is fucked up," he said in a deep, raspy baritone. His green eyes flickered under the light. "How is Cameron handling it?"

"He doesn't know," Brett answered solemnly. "I haven't done anything a recently widowed husband is supposed to do. I haven't contacted her family or made any arrangements. I mean, I'm at a fucking barbeque for Christ's sake. If it weren't already known how she had been killed, I'd be a suspect right now."

Anderson lifted his brow. "How are you supposed to mourn her? She was ditching you." Taking the pot off the stove, he emptied the food into a large bowl. "You know what you need to do? You need to go out there and pick one of those girls, take them into my bedroom and long stroke them. You'll feel better." He hit Brett on the chest as if he had just spoken the gospel.

"Don't listen to this dumbass," Joe said as a stern voice of reason. "How is *long stroking* some woman going to solve his problems, Anderson?"

"Once he gets some of the blue off his balls, he will be able to fix things. Right now, he's too fucked up in the head," Anderson answered.

"This is why he's been divorced twice," Joe said, hoping Brett didn't see any merit in what Anderson was saying. "He's an idiot. Been blown up too many times in combat. This mother fucker should be drawing down all 100% from the VA."

Anderson put up his hands. "How long has it been since you were laid?" he asked Brett.

Brett hunched his wide shoulders. "I don't know. Two months." He was lying. It had been three.

"Two months," Anderson said disappointed. "And you're married...were married?" He was in complete disbelief.

Brett lowered his voice to avoid anyone hearing him. "Yeah, Amy and I were having problems," he said a bit put off.

"You owe it to yourself," Anderson said slyly as he put his hand over Brett's shoulders. Pointing into the living room, he sipped on his beer. "Take your pick. There are short ones, tall ones, old ones, young ones. Whatever your heart desires. And you're a fucking grunt. Women love that shit. Hell, they put out and don't even expect a call back just so they can tell their girls that they've had a Recon man. What more could a single man ask for? Why take the job if you aren't going to enjoy one of the main benefits."

"The clap is not a benefit," Joe countered.

Brett's eye twitched. "I'm not single."

"You're not married anymore either. *Till death do you part,* man," Anderson said, winking his eye at a woman across the room who waved at them. "Oh, yeah. She's getting it tonight."

Brett raised his brow at Anderson's statement and sighed. While he had surely been an absentee husband most of his marriage, he had at least been faithful.   However, Anderson was right about one thing. He was single. And the reality of what being single meant both exhilarated and depressed him. The dating scene was not all that people made it out to be. If it was, then why did all his divorced friends constantly try to remarry again? There was something to be said about the institution of marriage as long as you weren't married to Amy.

Brett pulled away. "I'm going to step outside and have a cigarette," he said, leaving Anderson to sniff out the woman sending mixed signals across the room.

Joe had made his way to the grill. He was definitely not here for the women. With two plates in his hands, even after Judy had just cooked for them, he focused on adding on a few pounds and guzzling down free beer. Eyeing Brett as he made his way towards the beach, he raised his half-empty beer bottle to him, mid-conversation, and went back to filling his plate.

***

The tranquil breeze coming in from the roaring ocean seemed to calm Brett's thoughts. Cooling the sticky sweat around his shirt-collar as it whipped past him, he closed his eyes and felt the wind surround him. Funny how just one of God's many invisible forces made him feel so small and insignificant. Running the cold beer bottle over his hot skin, he pulled off his shoes and walked barefoot up the quiet trail, wiggling his feet in the wet sand.

For a moment, he was allowed to just think. A flash of Amy in her simple, white wedding dress came to mind, the smell of her perfume, the flicker of golden hair under her veil. He remembered when she was just an innocent girl with hopes of a blissful future. They used to lay in bed on a Saturday morning and talk about what it would be like to grow old together. He remembered how she would make him laugh with her spontaneous new hobbies or attempts at fame.

He recalled a few years ago when she had emerged from the shower soaking wet and covered in suds, proclaiming that she was going to be the next American Idol. They had driven two hours to Raleigh to tryouts so that she could sing her own rendition of Elvis Presley's Love Me Tender. He didn't have the heart to tell her that she sounded horrible. Instead, he had chosen to act surprised when she had emerged from the auditions with teary eyes and a bad (in fact dreadful) response from one of the judges.

Still, he had enjoyed her vitality, when she still had it. He never could put his finger on when they had lost their way. It was somewhere in between the cities of Iraq and the fewer and fewer calls he made home. Every time he called, she was more distant and he was more occupied. Towards the end of his last tour, he simply left messages on the voicemail. Amy had stopped picking up, claiming always to be out running errands. If he were truly honest, he had seen it coming. They had simply fallen out of love with each other, yet he didn't want to think that it could happen to him. He never thought that she would just leave.

Taking another swig of his beer, his thoughts quickly shifted. Anderson was right. It was most unusual that a couple so young would go so long without sex. He wondered if she had been in-volved in a sexual relationship with the Jermaine character from the phone. There had been so many accusations over the years. The rumor was that his Amy had a thing for officers. She always wanted him to be an officer, to go through the steps, to make the grade. She could never under-stand that he was happy being just who he was.

As the tide came rushing in, a figure in the distance pulled him from his thoughts. Carrying a purple surf board, a shapely dark-skinned black woman in a yellow bikini came out of the water.

In one arm, she carried her board and with the other, she ran her hand over her long black locks that spilled over onto her muscular shoulders.

He was walking directly in her path and stopped for a moment to make sure that his eyes weren't playing tricks on him. She was like a beautiful mirage in a hot desolate desert.

Throwing her board down, she pulled at the strings of her bikini and looked around. Planting her gaze on him, she raised her hand and waved. A perfect smile erupted from her lips revealing pearly white teeth.

He turned to look, making sure before he embarrassed himself that she was actually waving at him. Did he know her? Surely, he would remember her.

With a mean sway to her wide hips, she walked towards him, kicking the sand under feet. And with each devastating step that she took, she caused a strain in his heart. Her skin glistened even in the darkness. Confidence poured off her like the water that dripped from her moonlit hair. It was like he had seen an angel but without wings.

"Hey Marine," she said in an upbeat voice. "Funny seeing you here."

Brett squinted.

"Remember me from the library?" she asked, catching her breath.

As she got into full view, Brett realized that it was the librarian from Swansboro. His words caught in his throat as he watched her emerge from the blackness like a gift from God Almighty.

"Yeah, I remember you," he said in a deep baritone. His eyes lit up. She kept having that effect on him. Every time she was around, he felt lighter, *if there was such a thing*.

Wiping her face again, she looked up at him with her hands on her hips. "You live over here?" she asked, looking back at the party a few hundred yards away. "Or are you one of Anderson's friends?"

"You know Anderson?" he asked, raising his brow.

"Not in the Biblical-sense, no. I'm his neighbor...unfortunately." She looked back at her board. "I figured since he was going to keep me up with the racket, I might as well catch a few late night waves."

"Isn't that illegal?" he asked, looking at the intense waves as they came beating against the shoreline. She had to be pretty brave to ride those.

"Oh, isn't that cute. He's concerned." Turning away from him, she headed back to pick up her board. "I actually enjoy surfing at night. The moon, the wind, the peace and quiet. I don't know. It blows my skirt up," she screamed down the beach as she walked. It was like she knew that he wouldn't go anywhere, that he would stand at her feet like a lapdog.

"Let me help you with that," Brett said, darting in front of her. He ran down a few feet, picked up her things and turned to her. A pause in his words revealed his budding thoughts. "I'll walk back up with you. It isn't safe for you to be out so late."

"Well, there it is ladies. Chivalry isn't dead." Courtney smiled. She liked his concern, although completely unneeded. Nodding, she hunched her shoulders. "Okay, devil dog. Lead the way," she said, motioning down the beach.

Walking in-step with each other, Brett looked down at the perfect part in her curly hair and smiled. "You look different after work," he observed. It was the understatement of the year. She looked amazing nearly naked and soaking wet. Just the sight of her awakened his groggy libido. But there was something else about her that aroused his other senses, something unique to her and her alone.

"I guess you could say that I have a split personality," she answered of her late-night pursuits. "Did you find what you were looking for at the library today?"

"I actually ended up not needing it," he said, biting his lip. "She...uh...died today."

Courtney stopped walking. Alarm thickened the moment. Was she talking to a murderer? Did he come here to attack her for knowing that he had been researching a divorce?

Brett immediately realized how it all must have sounded or worse looked and quickly explained himself. "The big plane crash earlier today took her with it. It was all over the news. I didn't have any hand in it, if that's what you're thinking. Just ask Anderson. He hated her, but he wouldn't lie for me."

"Oh," Courtney said with a frown. She had seen the plane crash and there was no way to lie about that one. She quickly relaxed her tense shoulders and began walking again. "And you're out celebrating?" It still didn't seem right to her.

"No, just trying to figure things out." He looked into her eyes for approval. "Is that weird? Is it wrong?"

She blinked. "Depends. Where was she going on this plane ride?"

Brett couldn't help but notice her deep southern drawl. It was worse than his, almost Texaslike. All she was missing was a big cowboy hat and pair of chaps, which he wouldn't mind seeing her in at the moment.

"She was going to Japan to be with her lover," Brett finally answered after he pushed thoughts of her in leather chaps out of his mind. Anderson was right. He did need to get laid.

Courtney shook her head. "Ouch. Well, I don't guess I much blame you for needing to figure things out then. Sorry for your loss, just the same."

"Thanks," he said sincerely.

As they passed the growing crowd out on Anderson's deck, she pointed at the empty condo directly beside his. On the patio was a small umbrella covered table and hanging flowers with a small but very patriotic flag waving in the wind. It looked like a place for a single woman.

"That's me," she said proudly, reaching her arms out for her board. The gold bracelet on her wrist dangled in the darkness against her dark skin.

Brett passed her the board and smiled. "Thanks again for helping me earlier. It was nice to run into you. We should do it sometime again." He wanted to groan as soon as he said it. Was that the best he could do after so many years? Was that his best pickup line?

Courtney looked over at the crowd and frowned. "Would you like to come over and have a cup of coffee? I don't know you well, but that really doesn't look like your scene." She turned back and looked at him; her hazel brown eyes sparkled and sent warmness down his spine like he had just dipped his feet in hot water.

"Well?" she asked again, realizing that his mind had gone somewhere else. She moved her body into his view. "Do you want to come in?"

Brett was ecstatic that she asked. He counted back five seconds before he answered to keep himself from looking too eager. "Sure," he said, repressing a grin. "I'd love a cup."

"Good," she said, opening her patio door. Cold air rushed from her apartment into their faces. "Come on in. Make yourself comfortable. I'm going to throw on something more appropriate."

Chapter Four

Courtney's home smelled clean and fragrant like vanilla extract and shampoo. The small one-bedroom was whimsically designed with fresh daffodils in vases strategically placed around the living room to add color and accents of yellow and pink. Each lamp was an acrylic masterpiece shaped like a garden of bright flowers, making the place seem like a retro Tide commercial.

True to her profession, Courtney had lined neatly against nearly every wall tons of books – mostly classics. He didn't have time to check, but he was willing to bet that they were alphabetical. A huge picture of Jimi Hendrix was the focal point of the small living room right under a nostalgic yellow leather sofa. The floor was maple-colored hardwood covered by a green and yellow rug shaped like a patch of flowers. Over-all, it was unlike anything he had ever seen before. And it was refreshing to be in a house that had a personality, unlike his own house that was drab and lifeless.

When he realized that he had analyzed her entire apartment, he wondered if Amy hadn't turned him gay. What man paid attention to such things? The answer - a sexually suppressed man. Brett Black, king of the blue balls.

Sitting down on the diminutive yellow sofa, he nearly hid it with his size. It squeaked under his weight and the soft padding under him quickly deflated. Still, he sank down in comfort and rested his head back. A deep breath finally released from him and caused a strain in his chest. *Wow, this has been one hell of a day*, he said to himself.

Moving a multi-colored pillow from behind his back, he waited for her to come back out to join him. And for a minute, he wondered if this counted as a date. There were candles, a nearly naked woman and nice quiet apartment. This was something that he had not experienced in a while. It felt good, though it was on the eve of his wife's death. A tinge of guilt overcame him as he dwelled on how premature this makeshift date was. Life was a strange thing and often better than fiction.

Courtney didn't make him wait long. She sprang like a flower from her bedroom wearing a pink halter sundress that brought attention to the suntan lines on her dark shoulders.

Brett sat up a little, watching her every move. His mouth firmed involuntarily as he swept her body. Even in the dark, he could see her nipples pebbled against the soft cotton covering her skin. The first thought that came to mind was that she looked touchable.

"So do you want hazelnut or Columbian brew?" she asked, going to the kitchen.

Brett watched her as she popped into the kitchenette and opened up her pantry. Staring back at him with a smile, she waited.

"Columbian, please," he answered, wondering if she could tell he was attracted to her and wondering at the same time if she was attracted to him. Oddly enough, he wanted her to be.

"One fresh cup of *Columbian* coffee coming right up," she said, pulling a gourmet tin from the cabinet. As she did so, her damp hair fell over her face and suddenly Brett wanted to move it out of her way. He wanted to touch her soft as silk skin.

Her hazel brown eyes flashed at him before she went back to the task in front of her. That single moment of acknowledgement stung at him like a thousand bees. Was he supposed to feel like this? He could not explain it but she did something strange to him, something no other woman had ever done before.

With great effort, he managed to peel his eyes off of her and look around her place once more to calm himself. As she had hinted at, the music from Anderson's apartment banged against her wall. But inside her little safe haven, there was utter peace. After lighting a candle in the corner on the table, she brought over two cups of coffee and sat them down on the table in front of him.

"There you go," she said, bending over to put down the two paisley-colored mugs. The fleur-de-leaf golden necklace fell between her breasts and lodged itself against her firm orbs.

"Thanks," Brett said, sneaking a peak down her dress. She had full ripe breasts that made his mouth water. As she looked back up at him, he felt it in his groin. Desire.

Sitting across from him in a small chair, she put her feet under her and took a deep breath. "So," she said with a smile, "what does a man do when he goes from divorced to widowed?"

The question floored him. She was very direct. Rubbing his itchy, tired eyes with his index finger, he slumped down in the sofa and stretched out his long legs. "Well, I don't quite know yet," he answered honestly. "A lot has happened in the last twelve hours."

"Tell me about it," she said with a knowing nod. "I was told today that the county is cutting back and has to eliminate my job. So, I have to figure out another way to pay for my tuition. And I seriously doubt my parents will help."

Brett tried to focus. "Why?" he asked

"Because this is like my third try at it. I've changed my major too many times, and my dad hates indecisiveness. I went from wanting to be a doctor to a lawyer to a cop and now I'm going to become a librarian. Wait. That's four majors, isn't it?"

"Oh, you're a scatterbrain?" he frowned, wishing he hadn't said that. The last thing he wanted to do was offend her. She had been the only woman who had been nice to him in years.

Courtney laughed at his observation. Her light hearted giggle made him smile. "I used to be a scatterbrain. I went from Yale to University of Wilmington to the local community college. But what I always loved was books. So, once I realized that I decided that being a librarian would be best. I only have a year left in school. I actually stuck to his one." She said so with a grin, proud of herself and her accomplishment.

"Well at least you seem upbeat about it," Brett said, taking a sip of his coffee. "What did you do to this? It's great." The best coffee he had ever had or maybe it was because she had fixed it for him.

"Thanks," she said, watching his full mouth touch the mug. His features were striking to her, a strong chiseled jaw, tanned skin, piercing blue eyes, dirty-blonde hair, a straight perfect nose and naturally arched eyebrows. Was he a grunt or a model? She bit her lip. "I added a few special touches. I'm good at fixing coffee." Moving her hair behind her ear, she shook her head.

Why couldn't she stop flirting with him? It was driving her insane.

"Maybe you should change your major?" he said playfully. "Go into coffee."

Courtney laughed again. "At least you didn't lose your sense of humor." Her smile left as a thought crossed her mind. "How's Cameron?"

"Umm." He put down his mug. "You remember his name?"

"You sort of left an impression."

She is very direct, Brett thought to himself. He was impressed. "Cameron doesn't know yet." That was the second time that someone had asked him about how his son had taken the news. Maybe it was time that he told him.

Brett rested his head back on her couch and looked up at her ceiling fan. The chestnut-colored wooden blades turned quietly. "Like I said, I have a lot to figure out."

"Eventually, you're also going to have to mourn her, I imagine."

Brett looked over at her. "Eventually." His deep voice trailed off as his eyes started to close.

After such a long exhausting day, his mind and body began to involuntarily shut down on him. Plus, her place was inviting and warm. It begged for him to let his defenses down and rest. He did so obediently.

As the soft music played in the background and the candles danced about them in the darkness, Courtney watched him fall off to sleep. Slowly, his balled up fists relaxed. His large chest expanded with every inhale. Tight, perfect muscles lay rigid under his white Calvin Klein t-shirt. Shiny dog tags fell over on top of his beating heart. And Courtney, while looking at how peaceful he suddenly seemed, came to the realization that Brett Black was beautiful in a masculine sort of way.

Carefully putting down her coffee cup on the table to make sure it didn't make a sound, she went to her linen closet and pulled out a plush pink blanket, then carefully laid it over him. As she tried to put the pillow behind his head, his eyes shot open. Startled, his large hands shot up defensively and clenched her small waist.

Alarmed, she let out a gasp. Her long, damp hair fell over the two of them, smelling of shampoo and perfume.

"It's just me," she said in a whisper only an inch from his face. Her fingers rested on his wide, concrete shoulders.

His eye flinched. Adjusting his sight in the darkness, his gaze swept over her and recognized that she was not a threat – not in the normal way at least. He growled in a sensual low tone that made her rigid body go to liquid. Clenching her tighter as she relaxed, he pulled her in between his open legs.

Courtney was not shy. Her long dark arms wrapped around his thick muscular neck as she snaked her body into him. With hot breath hissed against his skin, she ducked in and stole a kiss from his parted lips. His hands quickly moved from her waist up her back to her shoulder and finally to cup her face.

Her mouth was warm, wet. He kissed her slow and easy. Searching it for every taste and every flavor, he pulled her to him, hungry for human interaction and was amazed by how good her body felt against his own, how soft the flesh inside her mouth felt as his tongue moved around it. She seemed to melt into him like they were meant to be. And for a moment, he couldn't get close enough.

Courtney had completely lost herself in him. Tilting her head to taste every part of his mouth, she felt her heart pounding against his chest. The smell of his cologne transferred from his body to hers. The kiss went from slow and easy to hard and passionate, igniting heat down in her belly and causing him to push his hips up to reveal his ramping need.

Straddling him while they kissed, she felt his strong hands as they cupped her bottom closer to him. His muscular arms bulged with pure power as he embraced her. Laying his head back, she fell into him deeper, kissing him faster. Another moan escaped, only no one knew from whom. He cursed in between their kisses as he looked down at her dress slowly easing down with all of the movement, barely hiding her breasts. Holding her small back in his hands, while the balls of his feet pushed up to help his knees arch her into his throbbing penis, he sank deep into her kiss, so deep until his burden did not feel as heavy anymore.

This was going too far. He wouldn't be able to control himself much longer. It was every part of her that drove him mad, her beautiful face, her enchanting body, her sensual smell, her soft touch. This room. The candles. The music. He wanted her more than he wanted to breathe at that very moment, and she wasn't stopping him.

"Easy," he whispered against her mouth as he panted. Exhaling a deep breath, he looked into her eyes. Unable to help himself, he kissed her one last time before he ramped it down. "You're...fucking amazing." His heart beat against her own. Her eyes were bright as she listened quietly.

"I don't know what happened," she said, moving her hair behind her ear. She sat up on him and pulled her dress up. Looking around dazed, she wiped her mouth. "That's never happened before."

He looked down at her still on top of him and rested his head back on the couch. "Unfortunately, that has never happened to me before either." His hands were still clenching her waist. Slowly, she moved and stood up. As she did so, he felt the strain of their distance. Cool air replaced the hot steam between them.

"What did you put in that coffee?" he asked with a frown.

Courtney laughed. "A little splash of happiness." Her bright eyes warmed his heart.

"I'm not stopping because I want to," he explained in a deep low voice. His lips were still wet with her kiss.

"No. We need to stop. I'm sorry. I...I am very attracted to you, Brett. But I don't normally behave this way."

"Maybe it's the stress," he said, looking away.

"Maybe..." she said, walking back over to him. Pulling the blanket over him, she kissed his forehead. As she did, he rubbed his hand over her back, unable to stop touching her.

"Get some rest. You're exhausted. I can see it in your eyes and I don't even know you," she said quietly.

"I'll just...rest here until my friend is ready to go," he said, feeling his eyelids grow heavy again. "You're house is like a freaking tranquilizer."

Courtney stepped away with a smile. "Shh...go to sleep."

***

The sun came creeping through the patio door to wake Brett from his hard sleep. As his eyes slowly opened, he looked around confused. Where was he? He sat up on the couch, tucked tightly in a pink blanket and realized that he had actually spent the night at the librarian's house. Jimi Hendrix played on the radio in the kitchen while Courtney cooked eggs and bacon and hummed to herself.

Throwing the food on a plate, she walked over to him. Now showered and dressed in a pair of khaki shorts and a pink polo, she placed his food down on the table beside a single yellow rose in a green vase that wasn't there the night before.

"Morning, sleepy head," she said with a smile. Her brow spiked at him. "Did you have pleasant dreams?"

"Morning," Brett said in a scratchy voice. "Better than that. I didn't dream at all." He looked down at his watch. 9:00 in the morning. Cameron! "Shit," he said, popping up. "I need to get to my son."

She looked up at him as he sprang from the couch and towered over her. He seemed even taller today. "Your friend, Joe, said he was taking him to his place. He came out on the beach calling for you just a few minutes after you passed out. I told him that you were sleeping. He said that you could pick him up this morning when you felt better. I didn't think that you would mind. You were exhausted – in no shape to watch a young child."

Brett sat back down, rested back a little easier and felt for his phone, but his pants were gone. He eyed them across from him laid carefully over the arm of her chair.

Courtney followed his gaze. "Hope you don't mind. I couldn't see how you'd be comfortable in those jeans all night. I mean, I sleep naked. So, I stole them from you last night. It was hard to do. You're sort of muscular."

Brett sucked his teeth. What else had she done while he was sleeping? He wondered if he had just dreamt that she'd kissed him or if last night was real. "Can you pass me my pants?" he asked, making sure to cover himself with the sheet. He had to pee and his morning boner was sticking up far enough to be noticed.

Courtney casually passed him his pants and nodded at his lap. "Nice to see you this morning, too, big boy."

He blushed as she turned away and went back to the kitchen. "Bathroom is down the hall to your right," she yelled as she banged around with the dishes.

***

After breakfast, Courtney drove Brett back west to Jacksonville to pick up his truck and Cameron at Joe's place. It was a short pleasant drive in her Toyota Tundra, decorated with flowers and smelling of vanilla. Brett didn't think the truck fit a woman at all, but strangely enough it fit her. With her surf board in the back and the music blasting, she wore a wide smile as she drove down the highway, looking like she didn't have a care in the world.

Brett had to admire her. She was not only beautiful but radiant. The sun had to compete with how bright she was, shining with every glance and every transparent smile. Even though he didn't know her, he swore that she had nothing to hide. Flashes of the night before passed through his mind. Her smell had transferred over to him and lingered on his clothes even now. He doubted very much that he would wash his shirt, just to keep the smell of her near.

"Was I drunk or did you tell me that you didn't have a job anymore?" Brett asked, turning down her radio.

"No, you weren't drunk," she said, looking over at him. "I'll soon be unemployed."

There was no worry in her voice. Again, he envied her.

Brett checked his phone. "Well, I'm going to need some help with Cameron. I was hoping for someone who could actually stay with me for a while. Would you be interested in the job? I'm sure that with the death benefit from the airline, I could afford to pay a lot better than the library. I live in Swansboro on East Ivybridge Drive. It's a nice enough place."

Courtney turned her lips up as she stopped at the red light. "Let me think about it," she said, turning to him.

"Okay, just let me know." He deflated.

"How can I let you know? I don't have your number?" She lifted her brow at him.

"I'll leave it with you. You can use it whenever you like, *even if you don't want the job*." He hoped that she would. It would be a shame to lose contact with her.

As the light turned green, Courtney turned her eyes from him and began to drive again. "Why would you ask me of all people?"

"Well, you work around children all day at the library, and Cameron seemed to have liked you." He felt like he was being interviewed. Shifting in his seat, he groaned. "And I like you." He looked over at her and found himself focusing on the dainty little mole on her neck.

In truth, he wanted to kiss her again right now to be sure that it was real. Her mouth had tasted like pure passion, like a woman with nothing to lose. He had never had that brand of woman before. It would be interesting to have *passion* again and to have her for the first time.

Courtney smiled. "You don't think that could be a problem? Me in your house like that? It sounds awfully convenient." She read his thoughts. "Especially after last night. Five minutes alone and we're all over each other."

"I can control myself," he said, looking out the window as he lied. "Can you?"

Courtney wouldn't lie. "Like I said, I'll have to think about it."

Brett chuckled under his breath. This woman was a real wild card. Shaking his head, he threw his arm out the window and tapped the top of the truck. "Well, like I said, just let me know."

***

Cameron was just a kid. How did someone tell a kid that his mother had just died? As they sat across from each other at the pizza place, while other kids played with their mommies and screamed and laughed, Brett watched his son with weary eyes. This was his Cameron's favorite place to eat. It only seemed right that he at least broach the subject here.

"How did you like hanging out with Judy and Joe last night?" Brett asked, taking a bite of his pizza. He locked eyes on him.

"It was fun. Joe Junior has a new Play Station," Cameron answered, sucking down cola.

"There is something that I want to talk to you about," Brett said, leaning into his son. "It's really important."

"Okay, daddy."

Brett swallowed hard. "You know how Momma went away yesterday? Well, she won't be coming back."

"For how long?" Cameron asked. His eyes were bright with confusion. It broke Brett's heart. *And people wondered why he hadn't broke the news yet?*

Choosing his words carefully, he ran a hand through his son's tousled hair. "She won't ever be coming back, buddy. But we have each other. I'll never leave you. I'll always be right here. And I know things are going to be *different* from now on, but I promise I'm going to do everything I can to make things comfortable for you." He knew his choice of words were lacking. He sounded like he was putting the boy in hospice, but this was the best that he could do.

"Why isn't she coming back?" Cameron asked with a whine, putting down his food.

Brett paused. *Did he really have to know the truth?* Wiping his hands on his napkin, he looked around the restaurant. "Because she went a long, long, long way away." He thought about the funeral. There would be no body. It meant that he would have time to explain this later, when Cameron could understand it, when it would be fairer for the little tyke.

Cameron frowned as he watched his father's face and the waves of raw emotion that washed over it. Sighing, he picked his pizza back up. "She'll be back," he said adamantly. "I know it."

The one thing that Brett had kept his son from for as long as he could had been death. He didn't want it to be such a real thing even though it had happened repeatedly around them. Brett's father had passed the year that Cameron was born; his mother had passed last year. His neighbor, who was another good friend of the family and a hell of a Marine, had been killed in Iraq last spring. Yet, Cameron had never been told about death. Now, he wished that he had something to refer to do – a dog, a fish, anything that kids could equate to the life cycle. There was nothing.

Good job, he admonished himself quietly.

"We'll talk about this again later on in life, okay sport?" Brett said, feeling himself choke up. He hoped that Cameron would give him some leeway on the subject.

"Okay, Daddy," Cameron said clueless. "I want to go and play on the slide," he said, getting up.

"Sounds good. I'll take you over there," Brett said, swallowing down his sadness. At least he still had him. And it was a much better trade off in his eyes.

***

It was an utter nightmare. As soon as Brett made the call to his mother-in-law, the drama began. Of course, Mr. and Mrs. Riley wanted to know the answers to a host of questions that he could not provide, like why she was going to Japan and why he didn't call the day before when he was first notified. He tried to keep his own feelings about them at bay while he explained as calmly as he could the order of events as ex-plained by the guy who came from the airline. However, he didn't have the finesse.

Mrs. Riley cried and screamed for her daugh-ter while her husband tried as hard as he could to find a way to blame Brett.

Holding the phone away from his ear, he leaned against the kitchen table and looked at their wedding picture. He was starting to feel less numb all of a sudden. In fact, he was starting to feel downright depressed.

"I'm making arrangements now for Amy. I just thought that Mrs. Riley might want to help," Brett said as he heard her crying in the background.

"We'll do what we can," Mr. Riley said with a sniffle. "Just tell me this. Why was our daughter headed to Japan?"

Brett huffed as he heard Mrs. Riley stop her crying to listen in on the explanation. "I think she was going to see a friend," he answered as he gritted his teeth. These people made him physically ill.

"You *think she was going to see a friend*?" Mr. Riley snapped. "That's an awfully long trip to make without knowing for sure where your wife was heading. Sharon doesn't go to the grocery store without me knowing about it."

"Well, I tried hard to give her the freedom she needed considering that I'm gone so much," Brett countered. He was painfully close to telling them that their daughter was a cheating whore, but for the minute, he held that bit of information.

"That's the problem with you kids and your damn new-fangled relationships. If you had put your foot down as the man of the house, she might still be alive," Mr. Riley said with cynicism lacing his words.

Brett rolled his eyes. "So this is my fault. I'm without a wife and my son is without a fucking mother and the only thing that you can say is that I should have been more of a man? When was the last time you grabbed a weapon and stood a post? When was the last time that you had to be real man *as you call it* or be responsible for the decisions of an entire country? While you were up in your pulpit singing praises to God on Sunday and burning crosses on Saturday night, I was on the front line with a fucking Sniper Rifle and unit of men who were willing to leave their entire families so that you could enjoy that fucking first amendment that you abuse with those bullshit dual-standard sermons that you push on unsuspecting people." His PTSD began to flare as did his nose. As his heart raced, he threw down the photo. "So, can your wife help me or not? There isn't much to bury, *as you can imagine.* I can just arrange for a short funeral here, or we can do something there in Fayetteville at your church. It's going to be up to you all. I don't really give a fuck."

There was a long silence on the other end of the line. His point had been made. Finally, Mr. Riley spoke. "We'll see to it that *our daughter* receives a proper burial and after that, I don't want to see you unless it's to see our grandson."

"You couldn't have given me a better gift," Brett said, hanging up the phone. He took a deep breath, tired of the many years of fighting with Amy's family over their closet-freak daughter. Her family had always blamed him for her many mistakes – her irresponsible spending, her tantrums and now her death.

Leaning his head against the wall, Brett closed his eyes and tried to stop the room from spinning. Heat and anger boiled over within him. Damn her! Damn her to hell!

Hitting his fist against the wall, he slid down to the cold floor and buried his head in his lap. His heart thudded in his chest, beating so loud until it deafened him as he broke out in a cold sweat.

Amy was dead. Amy was leaving him. Amy didn't love him. Those were not three opinions but three facts, and the new realizations were hard to swallow.

Embarrassed, he tried hard to hide his woeful sobs. The pain of trying to constrict his pain panged to the core of his broken heart. Cameron was in the next room watching television and finally seemed to be at peace. So, the last thing that he wanted was to let his boy see him in a state of panic. But the pain of his reality was weighing heavily upon him now.

Holding his hand over his mouth, he quieted himself and wiped the tears from his face. He had to keep it together, not only for himself but also for his son. He was depending on him now. There was no one else.

But why did it have to be that way for him? After all the work, after all of the sacrifice and pain, why did he have to be alone? Why couldn't he have someone to love him? Why didn't he deserve someone who shared in all of his dreams and his hopes? Why could he not be with some-one who appreciated who he was just as he was?

His questions were infinite and the more he thought about it, the angrier he became.

Pulling himself from the floor before he could dig into his own self-pity anymore, he wiped his face and looked up to the ceiling.

"I haven't spoken to you in so long?" he said aloud. "I was so angry with you because of Allen and the way that he died. I have been *angry* with you because of what you haven't helped me with. And I still don't understand you. I won't lie, but I'm asking you...I'm begging. Please God, send someone to help me," he pleaded.

The room was silent and still, like it had been extracted from the universe and hung in the balance of some different place. The slow drip from the faucet stopped.

The sounds of the television in the next room where Cameron sat quieted. Time itself halted.

He stood straight as a board, hands balled into fists, tears welding at the side of his red eyes, praying to the Being that he had turned away from during his last tour to a country that denied the very existence of his God and he waited.

Finally, exhaling a breath, he unclenched his jaw and dropped his shoulders. *What was he doing? Praying? Really?* He smirked to himself, nearly ready to give up, when suddenly his phone rang.

Digging into his pocket, he pulled out his Blackberry and was stunned. "Hello," he said in a deep, low voice.

"Hey Marine, it's me. I did some thinking, and I'm ready to accept your offer. When do I start?" Courtney said cheerily.

Brett was speechless. He looked back up at the ceiling confused. "You couldn't have called at a weirder time," he said, walking to his back door. He gazed out at his backyard and the inches of weeds that needed mowing down.

"Should I call back?" Courtney asked concerned.

"No," he said quickly. He released another sigh. "I'm glad you called. And I'm glad that you accepted my offer."

"I know that you don't have anything etched in stone yet, but after looking at all these damned bills that will be coming due after the next two weeks, I got to thinking and figured I better call before you hired someone else."

"The job is yours," he said, opening the door and stepping outside. Crickets chirped in the night. A calming breeze blew past him and cooled the heat that had begun to fester at his collar.

"Great. Well, I can't start for two weeks, but I can come there nights until this job ends."

"Two weeks is fine. I can swing it until then. Why don't we hook up next week? Right now, I've got some funeral arrangements that have to be made over in Fayetteville, but after that we can sit down and go over what I can pay you."

"Think I can get an advance?" she asked quickly. "I'd like to square away a few things."

"I don't think it'll be a problem," he said, willing to give her anything he had at that moment.

"Great. I'll see you then." She hung up as quickly as she had called. But the impact she had made on him was there long after her voice had trailed away.

Brett hung up the phone and shook his head. He never saw that one coming, but he didn't mind it. It was just what he needed to go back into the next room with his son and get through the night. Everything might be alright after all.

Chapter Five

After boxing up the last of her trinkets, Courtney looked at her watch and grabbed her purse. She couldn't be late for dinner at her parents' house. That always burned the old man's ass.

Turning off her lights, she glanced back at her small apartment, nearly all packed away and shook her head. Most people would be worried about making such a drastic decision (i.e. moving in with a family that they knew nothing about) but Courtney had a good feeling about Brett and Cameron, and she didn't believe in playing things safe. Unfortunately, that had been her downfall for most of her adult life.

She had bet everything on Mark, which had turned out to be a disaster. He had sailed off on a big ship never to return and married an Asian woman six months later. Word had traveled back to her in the form of a very informal email ending their relationship and her trust in sailors.

She had bet everything on Galen, which had turned out to be an even bigger disaster, when he ran off with her life savings and their dog, Butch. If she recalled correctly, he had a bit of a cocaine habit that he had hid very well until the end, though she should have been suspicious when her purse came up missing a few months into their relationship. However, he had always been great at sex, lying and avoiding creditors. More than her heart had suffered with him. Her credit score had crashed and burned. It was still recovering – slowly but surely.

Then she had bet everything on her father, when she had hoped that after Galen and Mark he might help her get back on her feet. Wishful thinking. Her father had turned his back on her and told her that both men, her poor credit and her decision to drop out of school was the last straw.

While her mother had secretly slipped her money to help along the way, it still took three jobs and evening classes at the local community college to get her back in the family's good graces and out of debt.

However, Courtney was still resilient even in the face of utter despair. She had always been like that. Since she was a little girl, she had never known exactly what she wanted in life, but she knew that she wanted to always enjoy the fullness of it. Thankfully, she had never been plagued with bitterness like many people that she knew.

For every time that something bad happened to her, she had been blessed with two or three great things.

Even now, she wasn't surprised when she was told by the library that it was downsizing. She was not surprised when she had met Brett. And she wasn't surprised when they found a way to help each other during their time of need.

In her mind, it was just the universe readjusting to take care of her.

However, her resilience wasn't always seen as a good thing by others. Her father had deemed her undependable and irresponsible. Those were his exact words.

As the only girl of two children, she had been the one who didn't seem to get *it*. Courtney agreed with her father on that. What was *it*? And why was *it* so important?

As far as she was concerned, the most important thing in life was happiness and without it, no matter how much money one had or how many titles one obtained, life was not complete. The people in her family, however, would highly disagree on any given day, especially Lieutenant Colonel Jeffery Lawless aka Old Man Lawless aka Daddy Hard-ass.

Courtney always thought that their surname simply didn't fit their family. Her clan was all about law and structure. Her father was a man who lived and died for principles that were based on honor, courage and commitment. And her brother had followed suit.

After graduating from Annapolis, David immediately took his place as an officer in the Marine Corps, making his father the proudest man in the universe.

Alternatively, she had failed out of her first year at Yale and found her way back home before the semester ended. Her father, of course, had been utterly devastated by her failure and found time to express his discontent at every single family function.

She had grown up on military bases around the world and was exposed to many cultures and people, except for her coveted summers, which were reserved for time with her grandma and grandpa in Austin, Texas, who had a flare for the eccentric and had a special place in their heart for their only granddaughter.

The *grampies*, as she affectionately called them, were a real God-send. They had accepted her just as she was and actually had a hand in her making. If it had not been for them, she may have crumbled under the demands of her father, but because of them, she had prevailed through his hellacious shit storms and often come out unscathed.

Loading into her truck with a green bean casserole that she had made for dinner, Courtney headed from her apartment in Emerald Isle to her family's sprawling villa in Indian Beach with a few minutes to spare.

She actually loved this community a lot more than any others her family had lived in before, which was why when she moved out of her parent's home, she had decided to stay close and move into an expensive little dive, too pricey for her pockets but close to her dear mother.

To say that she and her mother were close was an understatement. Courtney never let a day go by without calling her and never let a weekend past without seeing her. And because she didn't have any friends since she had moved back to Emerald Isle, her mom had to be her best friend, though she was certain that she didn't mine. Diane was a youthful woman with loads of energy and tons of optimism. Plus, she was glue that held them all together.

It was a peaceful night, just right for windows down and music blaring. The white yellow moon beamed down on her and illuminated the street lined with palm trees and gated homes of the coast's most prestigious families. The quiet tranquility of the waterway eased her spirit and put her at peace. Knowing what was ahead before she even arrived, she soaked up as much amity as she could before she pulled into the *colonel's* driveway.

A few short minutes later, she punched in the security code to the front gate and drove onto her family's expansive property. The Spanish-style luxury villa, complete with a red-tiled roof, expensive stucco and wood trim was situated on a cliff just 40 feet from the Atlantic Ocean. Palm trees lined the home on every side with a green plush manicured lawn illuminated by security lights that made the house seem even larger at night than in the day.

As Courtney pulled in front of the house, she parked her truck and looked up the stairs to the front double doors and took a deep, therapeutic breath. Home.

This was her family's seventh residence and more than likely, their last. Her father was due to retire soon. If he decided to finally rest instead of taking a job at the Pentagon, then her mother would get a chance to realize all of her decorative dreams.

While her mother always created a warm cozy home full of life and classic taste, she never fully committed herself to them because of the fear and knowledge that they would someday have to move. But when her father had announced that he might really retire this time, her mother devoted herself to this house, sparing no expense.

With the casserole in her hand and a bottle of wine in her bag, she hiked up the stairs and opened the doors to be received by the family dog, Benji. Bending down, she raked a hand over the back of the golden retriever and bid him good evening.

"What's up, mutt?" she said, closing her door with her foot. "Is anyone here?" she called out.

"In the dining room," her mother said, walking through the doorway. With a bright smile on her face, Mrs. Lawless came with open arms. She held her daughter tightly, savoring the feel of her prize possession before she took the food. "I'll take this to the kitchen. Did you use the recipe I gave you?"

"Sure did," Courtney said, looking around. "You've been working in the house, I see. It's really coming together." She noted the new tile recently laid in the foyer.

"Every day," her mother answered. "I'm going to Wilmington this weekend to pick up a few things that I found for the morning room. You should come if you aren't busy."

"I thought you said that you were going to wait until daddy decided for sure before you went crazy with this house."

"I'm hoping that I can *fully* persuade him," she said, walking into the large, open-aired kitchen. Placing the food on the island, she unsheathed the plastic covering and inspected her daughter's work. "Impressive," she said approvingly. "I can actually smell the onion powder. That is what gives it the kick."

"Why are you in such a good mood?" Courtney asked as she dug in the drawer for a corkscrew for the wine.

Mrs. Lawless let out a giggle. "Your brother is being transferred to Camp Lejeune. He'll be here in three weeks." She clasped her hands together and the huge diamond on her ring finger sparkled into Courtney's eye. "Now, I'll have both of my babies within arm's reach. It's a mother's dream."

Courtney paused. "It's a sister's nightmare," she said popping the cork on the wine.

David Lawless was a force to be reckoned with. As serious as his father and nearly as shrewd, her big brother was a testament to high society, while she was anything but. She had managed to keep a somewhat congenial relationship with him as long as he was far away at Camp Pendleton *whipping men into shape*, but the idea of him moving to Camp Lejeune was overwhelming.

Her father would surely be harder on her now, urging her to shape up and be more like her big brother, to focus on creating a better future for herself and no doubt urging David to find her a suitable match – an officer from a good family on his way up the military ladder. She gagged at the very thought.

"Well, aren't you the least bit happy?" her mother asked as she turned to lay eyes on her daughter. "He is your brother."

It wasn't like she needed to be reminded. "Of course I'm happy," Courtney lied. "Where is daddy?" Pouring a glass of wine, she passed it to her mother.

"He's upstairs washing up. He's been out in his shed tinkering around all evening," her mother said as she placed Courtney's food in a more suitable dish.

"What is he building now?"

"Oh, I don't know, child. That is the one place that I never go. It's his man cave."

Courtney watched her mother in envy. Dianna Lawless was a flawless beauty. With midnight skin as soft as silk, black hair streaked with silver and curled into soft tendrils, bright brown eyes and the most feminine features – a wide straight nose, full brown lips, heavy lashes under thick brows, perfect white teeth and a long, swan-like neck, she had been the cat's meow her entire life. As graceful as a queen and educated at Spelman, her mother had been a professional wife and mother that other military couples looked up to for decades.

"Why are you looking at me like that?" her mother asked, sipping on the wine.

She hunched her shoulders. "You're beautiful. That's all," Courtney said lovingly. "Daddy is really lucky." *And no matter how I try, I'll never be you*, she thought to herself quietly.

Diana smiled. "You are beautiful," she said proudly. "The most beautiful girl at Camp Lejeune." She sighed. "Have you told your father yet about your new job?"

Courtney smirked. "Are you crazy?"

"You should tell him, Courtney. Don't hide it from him. You're a grown woman now. You should stand by your decisions."

"Easy for you to say. You don't have to be his black sheep daughter. He's going to freak, Mom. I'm moving in with a white, enlisted widow to help raise his child. It sounds pre-emancipation."

Diana laughed. "It does, but you're doing it to further your education. You'll be a full-time librarian after college. It's a great profession and any man will be happy to have you as a wife."

"Any *officer*," Courtney corrected.

"There are other types of men in the world. As long as he is a good man, his profession does not matter." Diana knew that she was the only person in the family outside of her daughter who felt that way, still she felt as though she owed it to Courtney to stand beside her daughter's decision.

"Fine, I'll tell him at dinner. And then we can have an all-out war for desert," Courtney said with a grin.

***

The Lawless dining room had received some of the military's finest men and women as well as a host of dignitaries, philanthropists and local government officials. Diane had always been a devoted public servant serving at the head of her sorority for years, a member of local non-profit organizations and even as a member of the local historical society. She was the "it girl" and her husband loved it.

As such, the dining hall was a beautifully designed room right out of the Victorian era. Under a 19th-century chandelier and using a beautiful oak table from Spain as a the focal point, the accents of gilded gold and expensive wallpaper, art from Africa and serving utensils from England set the tone for fine living.

At the head of the table was Colonel Lawless himself. A clean-shaven, muscular man towering over the world at six foot four with piercing brown eyes and a commanding demeanor, the man of the house was a gentle as husband could be to a wife but as stern as a spinster headmaster over his children.

As he cut through his steak, he looked over at his daughter and then at his wife, knowing without knowing that something was on the horizon. "How is work?" the colonel asked, his deep baritone cutting through the silence like a knife.

Courtney looked over at her mother, who nodded in support. "Well, it's funny you should ask, Daddy. I have recently changed jobs."

The colonel's face stiffened. *How many times had he heard this before?* He waited for an explanation. The grip on his knife tightened.

Courtney patted her face with her napkin. "The library had to cut back on its staff due to the cuts in the budget. And my job was eliminated. So, I've taken a new job as a live-in nanny."

"A nanny?" The colonel asked appalled. "For whom?"

"A Marine who has been recently widowed. I'll be living with them for a while. The pay is really good, and it'll eliminate some of my bills and allow me to finish school."

"A Marine?" The colonel looked at his wife, knowing she had known about his daughter's decision for some time before him. "Is he an officer?"

"He's enlisted," Courtney said, bracing herself.

"Are you serious? You mean to tell me that *my daughter* is going to be working for an enlisted man in his house as *the help*?"

"You're being ridiculous now," Diane said, stepping in. "The point is that she has found employment and a way to solve her problems without us. You should be proud of her." She nodded at her daughter.

"Oh, I'm ecstatic," the colonel said sarcastically. He sucked his teeth. "Is he Black?"

"No," Courtney said quickly, looking down at her plate. Suddenly, she wasn't hungry. "Why can't you ever be proud of anything that I do, Daddy?"

"There are other jobs out there, Courtney." He heaved a heavy sigh. "Do you realize how this looks? It'll be all over the base. My daughter personally help set people of color back one hundred years in this area with a simple decision to become a house..."

"I could always be a stripper. Get a job at the Driftwood." She rolled her eyes. "This isn't about *you*. Everything is not about you!" Courtney exclaimed.

"Lower your voice in my house," the colonel demanded. His fists were balled around his plate, his jaw clenched. With a stern voice and glaring eyes, he snarled.

"Respect your daughter's decision," Diane countered in a low, calming voice. "And she's right. This isn't about you, *Jeffery*. We've already told her that we won't pay for her tuition. She's responsible for her own bills. It's not her fault that her job was cut. She did what any responsible adult would do. She found another job."

"I don't know why I even bother," Courtney said, standing up. "It would be easier to convert Fidel Castro into a Baptist republican than it would be to impress my own father."

The colonel looked over at his daughter and felt a tinge of compassion and guilt. Reaching out for her, he motioned for her to sit down. "Courtney," he said a little calmer. "What I'm simply asking you to do is look at it from my viewpoint. This is a serious blow to the family name."

"What have I ever done that wasn't a blow to the family name? This is exactly why I don't use it anymore. I don't' want to embarrass you." Courtney sat back down reluctantly, but she could feel her mother's stare – willing her to not walk away as she had done so many times before.

"This isn't permanent, is it?" the colonel asked, seeing his wife become uneasy. The last thing that he wanted to do was ruffle her feathers. And he knew how protective she was over her daughter. It was like a lioness and her cub.

"No, the job is only until I graduate and can find a position as a librarian. I'll even take a job in another state, if I have to."

"Well, I'm sure that I can find you a job on base. If you had only let me know..." His voice trailed off as he remembered telling her specifically to *grow up and handle her problems herself.*

"I wanted to handle this on my own," Courtney said, looking over at him for understanding. "I can look over my pride to accomplish my long-term goals."

"That's very mature of you, Courtney. We're both proud of you, and we will stand by your decision, won't we dear?" Diane said sternly to her husband.

The colonel nodded. "Yes...of course we will," he digressed in bitterness. It was useless to fight it anymore. The women of the house had made their decision, a bad one, but their collective decision none the less. *Lose the battle, win the war*, he said to himself as he picked up his fork again.

***

After dinner and Courtney had gone, the colonel and his wife stood in front of the kitchen sink carefully washing the wine glasses and listening to the jazz station. Under the dim light, he looked at his wife's delicate hands as they glided over the crystal and took a minute to appreciate how grounded she had always kept him. Passing her another flute, he scooted closer to her and looked down into her eyes.

"What would I do without you?" he asked in nearly a whisper.

"Fail miserably," she answered with a grin. She lifted her long lashes at him and raised her brow. "Are you flirting, Jeffery Lynn Lawless?" she asked in a deep, charming southern accent.

"I am, Mrs. Lawless," he said, taking a breath of her perfume. "Do you think I was too hard on her *again*?"

Diane smiled, showing the delicate lines of age around her full mouth as she did. "I always think you're too hard on her." Putting down the glass in her hand on the counter, she turned to her husband. "You know, we had to make our way. If I recall, your father wasn't too happy about you joining the military. His exact words were..."

"*A black man has no place in the military*," Lawless finished her sentence. "Yes, I know all of that."

"Well, could you imagine what your life might have been like if you had not joined, if you had listened to him? What I'm saying, dear," she said, easing up to him to put a hand on his chest, "is that you raised them and now you leave them to make adult decisions. They often know what is best; you just have to give them time to do what is best and not interject yourself into their lives. It's rude."

"Nobody complains when my interjecting saves the day. What about that other boy and his trifling dog? I found him and kicked his ass myself. And I never told a soul about that. I didn't gloat, though I wanted to. The boy handled himself like a nun. I beat his ass in four minutes flat. I didn't even get anything on me." He was proud of that considering he was suffering from a quiet mid-life crisis.

"Well, there were some benefits to you helping Courtney, but look at the draw backs. She lost a lot of self confidence in herself. That can irreparably damage a young woman. And it didn't help that you didn't allow me to tell her that the money was from you. She still thinks you're a tyrant, incapable of empathy."

Lawless's chest began to swell. "You think it's all my fault?"

"I think it's your responsibility to help her, not to harm her."

"I would never harm Courtney. She's my only daughter, and I love her more than life itself. It just drives me crazy to see her make such bad decisions. Now, do you mean to sit here and tell me that you're proud that she's now working for a *white* enlisted man as his help?" He put his hand on his hip as he awaited his answer.

"You're very blind, Lawless," Diane said, turning back to her dishes.

"How do you figure that?"

"Because anyone with eyes could see that she's not taking the job just for the money."

Lawless opened his mouth but quickly closed it shut. His eyebrow raised as thoughts assailed him. "You think she is..."

Diane shook her head. "I've said my peace. Leave her to make her own decisions."

He scoffed. *"Said your peace?* You've said nothing. You've just put all these horrible thoughts into my head."

Diane snickered. "Well, at least they are there. It's been ages."

"It's been since last week," he defended, forgetting about Courtney.

"Like I said, *ages*," she repeated with a naughty grin.

Colonel Lawless pulled his wife up into his arms and kissed her full mouth. Rubbing her backside, he moved her hair from her face. "Is that what all the fuss is about woman? Well, please allow me to remedy the situation." He growled at the thought, especially since he had already taken the little blue pill for later.

Diane laughed aloud as he grabbed her hand. "Where are we going?" she asked, holding tight to her position.

"Up to the room," he answered with a frown.

"No, Colonel Lawless. On the base, you are the final word. Here, I rule. And I say we do it *here*." Taking off her apron, she pointed over at the large kitchen table.

He cracked a smile and saluted her. "Yes ma'am."

Chapter Six

Early Sunday morning while families rushed off to church and ate breakfast around the table, Brett scurried around the house in a pair of yellow gloves, completing the last of his deep cleaning before Courtney arrived.

For the first time since he had moved into the house, he went through it with a fine tooth comb and inspected what needed to be cleaned like he was on the base during a barracks inspection. Not to his surprise, there were many things that had gone unchecked, like the dust balls in the corners behind every door, the dirty base boards, the closet full of dirty linen, the bottom of the refrigerator and the cobwebbed corners of the vaulted ceilings. His list went on and on.

On a mission, he had been up since three cleaning. However, to him it was well worth it. He didn't want Courtney to see the house in a mess, especially after seeing that her place was spotless. Now, it was near nine and he had spent six hours bent in crooked positions with scrubbers, sprays and other chemicals, but the end result was a more presentable home with a lot less clutter.

"Is she still coming, daddy?" Cameron asked, sitting in the living room with his eyes glued to

the front door. He had been waiting for Courtney the entire day, excited that someone new was
coming to the house.

"Yeah," Brett said exhausted. "She'll be here
any minute." Looking at his watch, he pulled his
disposable gloves off and went to the kitchen to
push them down in the overflowing garbage can.

That would be the last task of the day. He had
to get rid of all the evidence that told the story of
their unkempt house. With a quick spray of linen
air freshener, he pulled the black Hefty garbage
bag out of the can and tied it off then carted it
out the back door to the garbage can.

Opening the lid, he was greeted by the foul
odor of spoiled meat that had festered in one
hundred degree heat. Maggots stuck to the side
of the garbage can and fell as he dropped in the
bag.

He flinched a little, thinking of the carcasses
that were lined up and down the streets of Fallu-
jah during his deployment there a few years ago.
No civilian could imagine the type of larva that
oozed out of a dead body that had been out in
the heat for a few days straight. People often
walked passed them like it was common place
there, but he could never get used to it.

A quick flashback caused beads of sweat to
form on his head. Slamming the lid back shut, he
wiped his arm over his sweaty upper lip and took

a minute to breathe. The war seemed to never go away, and it reared its ugly head in the strangest of places. Brushing the thoughts off, he looked out across the half-acre of backyard and re-minded himself of something else he needed to do. It felt like he was always cutting the damned yard.

It was going to be a hot day, bright with a scorching sun and no clouds, perfect for throwing some meat on the grill. Just as the thought crossed his mind, he heard the hum of an engine in his driveway. Courtney. Looking over his gate, he saw her truck come to a stop and turn off.

Brett could feel his heart constrict when Courtney closed her door shut. Peeking over the top of his fence without being detected, he eyed her as she looked around at the houses, surveying her new home and hopefully approving of it. A single strand of hair fell out of her ponytail and flirted with the nape of her neck in the heat. Moving it out of her face, she threw her backpack over her shoulder and headed towards the front porch.

Brett quickly darted inside, letting the back door slam behind him.

Cameron was already screaming for him. With his little hand on the door knob, he tried desperately to open the door.

"Cameron, don't ever open the door without my permission," Brett admonished, moving him out of the way. The last thing he needed was for his son to wonder off one day. The thought made his heart skip a beat.

Opening the front door, Brett could barely repress his smile. Courtney, however, did not bother to hide hers. "Honey, I'm home," she said cleverly as she stepped inside. She brought the sunshine with her. The entire house instantly brightened up and everyone in it.

"Hey," Brett said, stepping back. He couldn't help but look her over. She looked effortlessly beautiful. "You're early. I was expecting you later." He lied through his teeth and prayed that Cameron wouldn't call him out on it.

"Well, I figured that I'd get a jump on the day," Courtney said, looking around his living room. "Wow, you have a nice place."

"Once I get you all moved in, I'll give you a personal tour," Brett said, taking her backpack. "Why don't I go outside and help you with your stuff."

Courtney nodded. "Okay." Dropping to her knees, she extended her arms for Cameron. "Hey you," she said as he ran to her. "How are you feeling today, buddy?"

"I'm hungry," Cameron said, giving her a big hug.

Brett winced. Shit. He knew he had forgotten to do something. Courtney looked up at him and raised her brow. "Mind if I fix him something to eat before we haul in my stuff?"

"I can do it," Brett said, feeling like he had dropped the ball.

"No, I want to do it. It's what I'm here for. Remember? Now," she said, standing back up. "where's the *cucina*?"

"Right this way," Brett said, leading her out of the living room. It had been a long time since a woman living with him was eager to get to the kitchen to cook.

As they walked through the house, Brett spied out the corners and rooms to make sure that everything looked picture perfect. It was odd to him that he even cared, but he wanted Courtney to feel as comfortable as possible.

"I can't thank you enough for doing this," Brett said, stepping aside to let her look over the kitchen.

She acknowledged that and then said, "I'm happy to be here. This is going to be great. Trust me." Her eyes found his and locked for a minute.

Brett couldn't quite explain it, but Courtney had a carefree, light heart that made him feel incredibly at ease. Maybe it was her lingering smile or her wide eyes full of hope, but it had been a long time since he had seen one person full of life. Plus, it didn't hurt that she was gorgeous. Her dark smooth skin looked as soft as silk and her fluffy black hair curled with heavy locks past her thin shoulders in a feminine way that turned him on. The twinkle in her brown eyes and curve of her tempting lips made him instantaneously think about their kiss. But he had made a promise. He had to control himself.

Courtney looked around the kitchen, opening cupboards and drawers. Going to the pantry, she opened it and put her hands on her hips. "We're going to have to go shopping." She looked back at Brett. "You okay with that?"

"You're not the maid, Courtney. You're his nanny. I can go shopping," Brett said, walking over to the cupboards to see what was so abhorrent about it. He looked in and sighed. *Shit again.* It was nearly empty with the exception of a large container of whey protein powder, a box of cereal, and a few cans of vegetables.

"See what I mean," Courtney said with a chuckle.

"I've just been so busy with him," Brett tried to explain.

Courtney put her hand up and silenced him. "That is what I'm here for. I'll fix him some cereal for now, and then you and I can make a list of things we need to stock up on later."

Brett liked the way that sounded, even if he didn't admit it. Being alone with Cameron, he had found out firsthand how hard it was to manage a house alone. There was a never-ending pile of dirty clothes in the washroom, dishes that always needed to be washed, a spill every five minutes on the floor, the boy was always hungry and never wanted to sleep alone in his room, and there was never a private moment where he could just relax.

Most days, Brett ran around in a daze with food spilled on his clothes and a washcloth in his hand, cleaning up behind Cameron and doing things he had married a woman to handle. Now thoroughly domesticated since Amy's death, the very thought of someone coming in to help brought him comfort that money never could.

It only took a few moments to unload the back of Courtney's truck. He noticed everything was color-coded in yellow and lime green stickers. Oddly, it made him think of a Sprite commercial. But it fit Courtney perfect. Bright colors for a bright person. She happily carted her things inside, placing them carefully in the entryway to separate the things going into his storage room apart from the things that would go with her.

"You ready to see your room?" Brett asked as he closed the front door.

"Sure," Courtney answered as Cameron curled up next to her leg. She looked down at him lovingly, already feeling a small bond growing between them.

Cameron looked up at her with a warm smile as if he knew something she did not. They gazed at each other for a quiet, brief moment sharing unspoken admiration.

Courtney was instantly moved. The poor little guy had gone through so much, yet he still had the courage to open his heart and try to love. The thought made Courtney wanted to give this job her best go at it.

Brett caught the exchanged between Courtney and Cameron but didn't speak on it. Who would have thought that he would end up in this situation? And while he was happy to have her here, he didn't have the luxury of such open fondness due simply to the sheer number of times he had been roughly disciplined for it. Exhibit A. *Amy Black.* The last thing that he wanted to do was set himself up for failure again. He would have to by any means necessary back off.

Clearing his throat, Brett breezed past them. "Your room's just up this way," he said in a low gruff voice.

His bottom foot hit the stairs with a thud, bringing Courtney out of her gaze. She followed him up, running her hand over the newly polished alabaster staircase as she glimpsed a view of his backside.

Brett's tight, muscular butt fit into his dark, denim jeans with ease and led down to his long, wide legs and the brown, quarter-length hiking boots that added a couple of inches to his already tall build. A faded gray T-shirt stretched across his back, clinging to his muscular form. And his high and tight haircut was *Marine Corps perfect*. Courtney definitely gave him an A for effort. It wasn't just the mood that night two weeks ago that had sent her into a frenzy.

Brett Black was hot every day.

He could feel her looking at him, and it damned near caused a stumble. He repressed a chuckle. *Weren't women supposed to have more couth?* When he got to the top of the steps, he looked back at her quickly and watched her eyes move up to his own. A smile quirked at his lips.

"I cleaned it as best I could," he said, opening the master bedroom door. He stepped aside and allowed her to step past him. "You have your own bathroom, a garden tub and shower, walk-in closet, bay windows that open for fresh air, a king-size bed, Wi-Fi, and you're right down the hall from Cameron."

Courtney looked around the room in approval. It was nearly empty, spotless and airy. The white-on-white furniture and walls gave the room a bright but lonely feeling, like something great had once lived here but had since gone away.

Brett leaned against the doorway, refusing to enter like crossing the threshold was his very own brand of kryptonite. With his large arms folded across his broad chest and pain visible on his sun-tanned face, he watched her as she sized up the room and his old life.

"Was this your room?" she asked, turning away from the window to look at him.

The sun caught in her brown hair and lit up her face. It was a warming sight for Brett, so he answered truthfully.

"It used to be...once upon a time." His rugged voice cared the hum of a country music singer and the pain of the blues.

"And you don't mind me sleeping in here?" she asked, walking towards him. "You don't have a guest room?"

Brett's crystal blue eyes twitched. "No, I don't mind." He swallowed hard. "I don't sleep here. I normally crash downstairs in the den." Nervously, he scratched the back of his head. His bicep bulged again as he did, drawing Courtney's attention.

"I like it," Courtney said finally. "It's a beautiful room. Thank you."

Brett nodded, relieved that that was over. "Good. Well, let me know what you need to make it more *like your own*, and I'll get it for you. I have to return back to work tomorrow. So, I'll stop by the commissary and pick up some stuff."

Courtney raised her brow, noticing he avoided any conversation about Amy's death or how it made him feel. Evidently, he was a man of very few words, *maybe too few*, but she'd change that soon enough.

Brett could see that she was thinking something clever, but he did not want her to get any ideas. He looked down and realized that she had moved all the way from across the room and was now right in front of him. Her smell wafted up to his nose, familiar and sexy. Taking a deep breath, he shifted gears. After all, he had promised her that he could keep things Kosher between them. No point in ruining things on the first day.

"Well, I'll help you get everything moved up here, now that I know that you like it," Brett said, looking at the shape of her lips. His breaths quickened slightly.

"I'll help you," Courtney said, stepping past him and Cameron, who stood behind his father's leg listening.

Brett growled as she passed. This was going to be harder than he thought. He had to be crazy moving her in here as vulnerable as he was, yet he knew that he needed her more than he wanted her.

He looked down at Cameron, who watched him carefully and shrugged his shoulders.

"Do you like her?" he asked his son under his breath.

Cameron smiled and looked down the stairs. "Yes," he said with a giggle. "So do you, Daddy."

Courtney smiled as she hit the bottom step. Strange thing about acoustics. They carried every sound. But she was glad that Cameron liked her. She liked him too. Only, she liked Brett a lot more.

***

Sunday evening at Camp Lejeune was bustling with people. As the sun set on the horizon, Brett and Courtney drove down the main road with the windows down and music low. Cameron sat in the back playing with his toys and staring out of the window.

On the sides of the road, people took their late evening run or walk, many with children trailing behind them or in front of them in buggies. The thing about enlisted and officers alike was the huge family syndrome. Due to lonely wives and serial deployments, many couples chose to insulate themselves with multiple children to ensure the family line or simply ended up with surprise pregnancies after a long time apart.

Courtney looked out of the window at the passing people while the wind jetted through her hair. With a smile on her face, she quietly sat in a peaceful daze that made Brett envious. He looked over at her and shook his head.

"Why do you always look so happy?" he asked, making eye contact with her.

Courtney trailed her finger over the side of the dashboard. "I imagine it's because most of the time I am happy."

A faint grin twisted his lips again. "But why?"

"You know, I've been asked that my entire life. And the truth of the matter is that I don't know. I was just born happy." She smiled at Brett.

Brett frowned. "But you're not *always* happy, are you?"

"No. I'm not always happy. I've had some pretty shitty times before, but the bad doesn't outweigh the good, and that is what is important."

Brett chuckled. "You sound like that purple dinosaur right now."

Courtney couldn't help but grin. "Are you happy most of the time?"

Pulling into the commissary, Brett parked the truck and turned it off. Turning to her, he looked into her hazel eyes and sighed. "My life has been a comedy of errors, Cort. Some parts of it have been happy, but most of it hasn't been. I've experienced the whole spectrum of emotions from happy to psychotic."

"And does my happiness offend you?" she asked seriously.

"No, it just intrigues the hell out of me...that and wondering what kind of accent you have."

Courtney laughed. "I can't believe that you've already given me a nickname. *Cort?* My grampies call me Cort."

Brett glanced at her lips as she said the words. "Where are they?" he asked, leaning further over to her.

"In Austin, Texas. I used to visit them every summer when I was a girl. That's probably where the accent comes from," she said, feeling nostalgic. "Are your grandparents around?"

Brett nodded. "Not for a very long time." He pulled back a little as he felt himself drifting off towards a kiss. "Okay. We're here. We've got an hour before they close. Think you can go hog wild with your list before then?"

"I don't know. Cameron, you feel like helping me shop?" Courtney asked, looking back at his son.

"I want cereal," Cameron answered with a big smile.

Brett laughed. "That boy *loves* cereal."

"Are you coming in?" Courtney asked, opening the door.

"Yeah, I have to. You have to have a military ID to check out."

"Oh, I have one," Courtney said, pulling out a military ID from her pocket. "Since I'm *still* in college, I have to use a dependent ID from my father."

"Your father's military? Is he retired" Brett asked, reaching his hand out. *She had not mentioned that before.* "Let me see."

Courtney hesitated. "Just don't freak, okay?"

Brett frowned. "Why would I freak?" Taking the blue, laminated ID out of her clutches, he read the sponsor's name and rank and turned pale. There were no words to express his sudden shock. His nanny was also the daughter of his Lieutenant Colonel. Shit!

Passing the ID back to Courtney, he felt his mouth spasm as he dragged in a breath. "I thought you said that your name was Redbrook?" he asked, wiping his brow.

"That's my mother's *maiden* name. I've been using it since I graduated from high school, and I guess you know why." She offered him the bottle water in the cup holder. "Brett, it's not a big deal. He knows that I'm working for you. Well, not you. He knows that I'm working for a Marine."

Courtney couldn't name the number of times that she had gotten the exact same reaction from people because of her father. It was why she had chosen to withhold the information from most. There were automatic assumptions that she didn't want, but always nearly received.

"Oh, that's wonderful," Brett said sarcastically. "As if my life couldn't get any more complicated, you tell me that you're Lawless's daughter? Do you know who this man is? He's like Zeus's right hand. This man went Recon when it wasn't even cool for Black men to even apply for Special Forces. He still holds some serious records in dive school and on the shooting range. You can't get more hardcore than your father used to be before he *ascended* up the ranks. Plus, he's my fucking battalion commander, Courtney," he moaned. "Why didn't you tell me?"

"Because you wouldn't have treated me the way that you have," she said sincerely. She leaned into him.

"And how have I been treating you?"

"I don't know," she shrugged her shoulders in frustration, "like a normal person. You would not have hired me if you had known my father's last name."

Brett quietly agreed and still wondered if he shouldn't just call the whole thing off right now. "How does he feel about you working for me?"

Courtney smirked. "What does it matter?"

Brett's eye twitched. "What does he think?" he asked sternly. His eyes locked on her for an answer.

With a sigh, she turned her head from him and stared out the front window. "My father has never been happy with *anything* that I've done. And I didn't disappoint this time around. But it is not about what he wants for me. It's about what I want for me. And I want this job, or I would not have taken it."

Watching her quietly, Brett could see her growing agitation. Evidently, he had hit a sore spot with her. Still, he had his reservations. Sitting back in his seat, he rested his head back and closed his eyes. The mood had just changed from *happy* to heavy.

Courtney waited silently for him to say something, but Brett sat still with his lips pursed together. Giving up, she opened the door. As she stepped out, she felt his large hand grab her other hand. Slowly, she looked over at him.

"I didn't mean to make you sad," he said gruffly. Letting go of her hand, he sighed. "I just don't want any trouble right now. And I'm not talking about school boy scared here. I'm up for promotion. And I have a child to take care of."

Courtney could understand the position that she had put him in, but desperately wanted him not to give up on her. "I'm a grown woman, Brett. My father has no bearing on this relationship. And I assure you that I won't get in the way of your promotion."

Brett paused. She had taken the words right out of his mouth. While they were not dating, they did have something more than just an arrangement, and he did not want to see her sad before they could even build on what was going on between them. Nodding, he sucked it up. "It could be worse, I imagine. You could be seventeen."

Courtney laughed. "I'm twenty-two years old."

Brett looked into her eyes and felt like her soul was much older and wiser. Everything she had done up to this point had been mature and thought out. He had to give her the opportunity to be more than just her father's daughter. Yet, he knew that he had to tread carefully.

"No complications," he said, looking back at his son. "For his sake, I can't afford it. I've already had to deal with one daddy's girl, and it was sheer hell from the beginning."

"I'm your nanny. What's complicated about that?" she asked with a smile.

Brett smirked. "Have you seen yourself lately?"

"You think I'm beautiful?" she asked playfully.

"You damned right," he said with a sexy southern drawl. "That's why I'm warning you. We need to be *very careful*."

"I told you when I started this that I can control myself. The only complication will be you, Brett Black." With that, she stepped out of the door and closed it behind her.

Chapter Seven

Four o'clock in the morning came early for Brett. His eyes flashed open from a nightmare that had him covered in sweat. Sitting up on the couch, he ran his hand over his shaved head and grunted. *Fucking Iraq.* No matter how long it had been, he still had the same dreams of being shot in the face while on patrol.

The room was pitch black with only the sound of the box fan blowing directly on him. Turning on the lamp, he looked at his watch and turned off the alarm on his cell phone before it went off.

Back to work. He had been off long enough, now it was time to return to the real world and Courtney's father. He had gone to bed the night before thinking about what he had gotten himself into. There was no way that he was not going to have to face the man at some point, and he was sure that when he did, Lawless would have a few words for him. But he'd just have to cross that road when he got to it.

Dragging himself out of the den, he headed to the bathroom and noticed that the kitchen light was on. The smell of fresh coffee and breakfast filtered throughout the house. Looking down at his morning boner, he decided to investigate *after* he came out of the bathroom.

Courtney had been up for nearly thirty minutes. With the kitchen television on the news, she flipped hot pancakes on the stove and thumbed through her textbook.

She had always been an early riser, mostly because in her house as a child, it had been a sin to sleep in. Acclimated to the Marine Corps now, she rather liked getting a start on her day early. It allowed her to accomplish more and to get to bed earlier.

"Morning," Brett said from behind her.

She turned from the television and looked over at him. "Morning," she said, noticing him in white boxers and nothing else except his dog tags. His muscular body was covered in tattoos. After a quick glance, she turned back to her food. Evidently, he didn't have plans to make things easy on her.

Brett was not without his own observations. Covered in a yellow, short kimono with her hair pulled up in a clip, Courtney looked more like a wife than a nanny. She stood at the stove with one foot wrapped around her long leg relaxed and pleasant. Pouring a cup of coffee for him, she offered it.

"Hope you like French Vanilla coffee. I grabbed the wrong one at the store last night," she said as he walked up to her. She looked up at him and noticed the perfection of his square jaw.

Brett took the coffee and resisted the natural urge to bend down and kiss her full lips. "French is fine. Thanks," he said in a deep baritone. "You always get up this early, or are you trying to impress me?"

"Did you forget who my father is?" she asked playfully.

"Point taken," Brett said, sitting at the table. "I'm not used to being served breakfast unless I am at a restaurant. So you'll pardon the shock."

"Oh, you want some of this?" she asked, fixing his plate.

Brett thought the question could easily have two meanings, but he played it safe. "If you don't mind."

"I'm just kidding with you. Of course, I fixed you breakfast. You can't go training without it." Putting down the plate of pancakes, sausage links and eggs in front of him, she rubbed the top of his head. "Did you sleep well?"

"No," he answered as he pushed the chair back to get silverware.

Courtney quickly passed it to him. "Why not?" she asked.

He took the fork and knife. Pausing, he raised his brow. "I have...nightmares."

"PTSD?"

Brett scratched his stubby beard. He'd get rid of it after breakfast. "Yep," he answered flat and hard. "I'm supposed to go to see this base shrink, but the guy is full of shit."

"I've heard that before," Courtney said, fixing her own plate. She sat down across from him and looked down at her food. "Do you want to bless the food?"

"No, you do it."

Courtney bowed her head. "Thank you, Lord, for the food we are about to receive. Let it edification for the mind, body and soul. And please help Brett with his nightmares. Amen."

"Amen," Brett said, raising his head. He stabbed his food and tasted it.

She waited. "You like?"

"Umm," Brett said with a mouth full of food. "It's been ages since a woman fixed me breakfast at four in the morning."

"And you didn't even have to sleep with me. Isn't paying for it great?"

Brett chuckled. He'd pay for *it* alright.

"Cameron and I have tons to do today. I saw on the list that he supposed to go to the pediatrician. So, I'm going to take him there, and then we're going to the park, the library and the bookstore."

"Sounds awesome. I'll leave my bank card." He shoveled more food in his mouth.

"What time do you normally get home?"

Brett bit his lip. "I don't ever know. Most of the time, I get here by six or seven. I'm normally the last to leave."

"Why?"

"Excuse me?" The food stuck in his throat.

"Why are you the last to leave?" Courtney repeated her question comfortably.

Brett frowned. "I'm a squad leader."

"You mean that you hate coming home," Courtney answered for him.

He didn't know how to answer, even though he knew that she was right. Was he that transparent? Smacking his lips together, he put down his fork. "You don't hold back, do you?"

Her voice was tranquil and sweet. "No." She stared into his eyes.

Brett conceded. "I normally go and grab a beer off base and get my thoughts together before I come home. It's out in Jacksonville. So, I tend to get home at about seven."

"Fair enough. I'll see you then," she said, sipping her coffee. "Now, wasn't that easy?"

Brett picked his fork back up. "Easy for whom?"

Courtney smirked. She had known enough Marines and lived on the base long enough to know that when a grunt got off work for the day, he busted his ass getting off base. If he didn't, it was normally because he was avoiding his family like the plague.

Her father had drug his feet after early deployments when she was little. She vividly remembered her mother confronting him on several occasions about his constant tardiness. It was then that she decided as a young child that marring a Marine was simply out of the question.

***

When Brett came out of the den fully dressed in his desert uniform, his boots laced to the top with his boot bands on, his cover down on his head and his assault pack thrown over his arm, Courtney almost gasped aloud. She had seen a thousand Marines, but the look of him in his uniform was purely a guilty pleasure.

Brett hardly noticed when her eyes lit up. With his head down, he walked into the kitchen and grabbed his lunch, then looked at his watch.

"Gotta go," he said, turning to her. He almost kissed her again, yet he couldn't understand why it seemed so natural. Her smell kept enticing him; her pouty lips and fresh face bright with expectation kept calling out to him. *This is going to be hard*, he thought to himself as he nodded at her.

"Have a great day," she said, closing her textbook.

"You too," he said, stopping at the door. "If you need anything, you can call me on my cell."

"I'll be fine," she said with a smile.

***

The Naval Hospital was packed by noon. With Cameron in his stroller, Courtney strode into the pediatric center with a backpack full of pull-ups, baby wipes, lunch and water and checked in at the front desk. She noticed a few stares as she did so. Black woman. White kid. Who said racism was dead? Smirking, she pulled Cameron out of the stroller and pointed him toward the play center.

"Go play, baby," she said lovingly as she kissed the top of his head.

Unaware of his surroundings, he ran over to play with the other kids while she waited for their name to be called.

The other women sitting in the waiting room - both black and white - spied her as she flipped through her book. Cameron was a brunette boy with fair skin, brown eyes and rosy cheeks. Courtney was in contrast dark-skinned. It was a curious sight, she knew. Yet, she became quickly agitated. Closing her book finally, she crossed her legs and looked over at the women across from her.

"It's not nice to stare, or didn't they teach you girls that at charm school?" she snarled.

The women quickly looked away, making Courtney laugh aloud.

***

Shots of any kind were never good for children. Holding Cameron tight, she tried to keep his attention while the nurse pulled out the needle. Only Cameron had suffered through shots before and knew what to expect. He immediately began to cry loud, screaming for his *mom*. The sight hurt Courtney to her heart.

Holding him close to her bosom, she felt him flex his muscles tight and cry out. She wondered how much screaming was due to the pain of the shot versus the pain of his mother's absence. Who would do this to a kid? What kind of woman would run off and leave her only child? *Serves the bitch right to be dead,* she thought to herself as she comforted Cameron.

"There, there now. You have to get your shots, baby. You want to go to school and play don't you?" she asked, kissing away his tears.

"I want my mommy," Cameron cried. "Where is my mommy?"

Courtney didn't answer. The nurse looked at them with a quiet nod. Word had gotten around about what had happened to Amy. Only, they did not know the specifics. So, it looked like either Brett had gotten help for a while, or he had already moved on.

Taking the paperwork from his physical and placing it in the baby bag, she put him in the stroller and gave him a Popsicle.

"You can take that form with you to the base pre-school and get him registered," the nurse said to Courtney with a gentle smile. "But you'll need Staff Sergeant Black to be present."

"Oh, he gave me power of attorney. I'm good," Courtney said, pushing Cameron out of the room.

The nurse looked flabbergasted. Power of Attorney? Evidently, the Staff Sergeant *had* moved on.

Breaking out of the hospital in the heat of mid-day headed towards the truck, Courtney pulled her ball cap down on her head and tugged on her ponytail. Even though Cameron wasn't her child, she suddenly felt horrid for him and for Brett. But what more could she do than what she was doing?

Brett had asked her to get Cameron into pre-school for three days a week to help him learn to deal with his loss and to keep him from becoming anti-social. The therapist had made that recommendation after their first session, which had also been their last. Brett had told Courtney that the only good thing that had come out of the session was that suggestion and nothing more. He had even referred to the female doctor as a *meddler*.

Courtney chuckled. Men were pigs. Still, here she was with this child who definitely had suffered through the loss of his mother and was now missing the loving kisses and touches of two parents. There had to be something to cheer him up. Getting an idea, she snapped her fingers.

"Hey, do you like water?" she asked as she put Cameron in the truck.

"Yes," he answered with teary eyes.

"Wanna go to the beach?" she asked.

He shook his head with a bright smile. "Can I make a castle?"

"You can make whatever you want to make. Just let me get you enrolled in this little school for *super cool* kids and then we can go to the beach and hang out for a while. Does that sound good?"

"Yes," Cameron said, sniffling. But at least she had gotten a smile out of him.

"Great." Courtney closed the door and leaned against it.

Poor little guy. She couldn't imagine what he was feeling. She had never lost anyone before. Her grampies were even still alive for goodness sake and they were ancient. Yet here was Cameron, just a little child, and he had lost one of the most important people in his life.

It was tragic and uncalled for. It made her think of her own mother and how kind Diane had been her entire life. There wasn't a single memory in her childhood that didn't include her mother in some kind of way. She was always there, always protecting her and guiding her, especially when her father was away. It was strange how something tragic had to happen to someone else for her to see how blessed she had been. It made her want to call her mother right then and thank her.

**

At exactly four thirty, Brett was finished with work and was now utterly exhausted. After a five-mile run and two hours at the shooting range along with operational training, all he wanted to do was take a shower, have a beer and relax.

Returning back to work had actually not been too bad. For one, he didn't run into the colonel. Secondly, he actually enjoyed not spending his day coordinating funerals and taking care of Cameron. He was a grunt, made for the field. And the time away only confirmed it.

Throwing his backpack in his truck, he loaded up and headed towards the house. Normally, he would have stopped and had a drink with Joe, but today, he decided against it. It could have been just the fact that Courtney had brought it up that morning, *which was very awkward*. Or it could have been that he really wanted to see her. But whatever it was, today was the first day in a while he had felt like going home.

***

Courtney had just finished fixing dinner. As she placed the salmon and avocados down on the table by the red peppers, rice pilaf and wine, she heard the front door close shut. As soon as he heard him, Cameron jumped down from the table and met Brett at the door with a big hug.

"What's up, big guy?" Brett said, rubbing his back.

"We went to the beach," Cameron announced.

"I can see that. You got quite a tan," Brett said, rubbing the top of his head.

"And we went and saw Courtney's mom. She's really nice, and she fixed me muffins. But she wouldn't fix me cereal."

Brett stopped. His son was at the colonel's house today? Sighing, he debated whether or not to speak about the matter. On the one hand, it gave Cameron more interaction with people. On the other hand, it broke down the barriers between his house and his commanding officer, which could potentially be a problem down the line.

"Hi," Courtney said, walking out of the kitchen.

"Hi," Brett said, forgetting his train of thought. She looked amazing in her jeans and V-neck T-shirt that showed off her ample cleavage. With a smile, she removed the mitten from her hand. "How was work?" Her hazel eyes beamed at him.

"It was good...to be back," he said with a smirk. There was no way he was going to mess up the evening by arguing over Courtney's mother. "You cooked again?" he asked, smelling the food.

"I figured that you'd be hungry," she said as Cameron walked over to her. "Hope you don't mind."

"I don't," he said, dropping his bag. He could get used to this real quick.

"Great. Dinner will be ready in about five minutes." She turned back around and headed back into the kitchen.

"I'll go wash up," Brett said quickly.

***

The hot water felt good against his skin. Leaning against the tile, Brett rested his head down in the stream and let it run down his back. Steam fogged up the bathroom and created a haze around him. Relaxed, he washed his hair and released the tension from his body.

He could let his guard down finally. It was a force of habit to be rigid – something he tried hard to leave at work but sometimes failed to do. At the base, his guard had to be up. He had to pay very close attention to detail, focus, train hard and worry about his squad.

Recon was not an easy job. It required extreme discipline, die-hard dedication and the ability to go numb when necessary.

The problem was remembering when to turn the grunt on and when to turn him off. Often Brett felt like he was in limbo, hanging somewhere in between the two men he was forced to be on a daily basis. With Amy, it was even harder to handle. While she had never been diagnosed with bi-polar disorder, she had all the symptoms with her manic highs and lows that went on for days at a time. The combination of his profession and her impatience made for a bad marriage all around.

But Brett couldn't think about that now. There was food waiting for him downstairs, prepared by a beautiful woman who was taking good care of his son. He didn't have to argue about money or bills or men. He didn't have to have his guard up, and he didn't have to be someone else.

Five minutes later, Brett was sitting at the table with Cameron and Courtney laughing so hard until his eyes were watering. Evidently, she had taken Cameron out to catch a few waves and during the process, he had lost his trunks. As Courtney retold the event, Cameron turned bright red and couldn't stop blushing. But he was also not deterred. He liked the beach and swimming off shore so much until he wanted to go back tomorrow.

"Oh, that reminds me," Courtney said, going to her backpack. "We went and had our shots today."

Cameron frowned at the mention of it. "It hurt really bad, daddy," he whispered to his father.

Coming back to the table, Courtney passed Brett the paper. "I filled out the forms for pre-school and got him registered, but I wanted you to look over it and make sure that I listed every-thing correctly, especially emergency contact information outside of myself."

"Thanks," Brett said, taking the paperwork. Licking his fingers, he looked up and caught Courtney giving him an admonishing glare about his bad table manners. "Give me a break," he said playfully as he flipped through the papers. "Everything looks fine with the exception of the blood type. It says AB negative. This is wrong - impossible actually because I'm O positive and so was Amy." He looked at Cameron as he made the accidental slip up of mentioning her name.

"Oh, sorry. I took it from his physical. They have it listed on his paperwork," Courtney said, putting more salmon on Brett's plate.

"What?" Brett turned to Cameron's physical paperwork and read it carefully. "Well, this can't be right," he said under his breath.

"What? Did I do something wrong?" Courtney asked as she poured Cameron some more juice.

"No." Brett frowned and stood up from the table. This had been the first time in Cameron's short life that someone other than Amy had taken him to the doctor. She was always adamant about doing so alone. With the paperwork still in his hand, he headed out of the kitchen. "I'll be right back," he said in a daze.

Courtney looked over at Cameron and raised her brow, but did not give much thought to him stepping away. Maybe the food was messing with his stomach. She had made a spicy pineapple chutney topping to go with dinner.

Brett went to their cabinet in the den and dug through Cameron's files. Pulling the physical from his 12-month checkup, he looked at the blood type. AB Negative. Going to his birth records, he thumbed through the paperwork to find his blood type. AB Negative.

"How could I be so fucking stupid?!" Brett screamed as he stood up. Kicking the desk, the chair fell over, and he had to yank his foot out of the drywall. Courtney heard his outburst and looked down at Cameron, who immediately tried to get up and run to him.

"No," Courtney said, grabbing Cameron by his little arm.

"But what's wrong with daddy?" Cameron asked alarmed. He looked back towards the door, trying to pry away.

Courtney recalled their conversation and suddenly it hit her. "Oh my God," she said, putting her hand to her mouth. Looking over at the boy, she rubbed through his hair and tried to smile. "Are you finished eating?"

"Yes," Cameron answered.

"Good. I'm going to take you up to your room and get you ready for bed. It's late now."

"But I want to say goodnight to Daddy," Cameron pleaded.

"Your father needs a minute," Courtney said with a heave. Picking him up in her loving embrace to ensure he didn't run into the den and see his father mourning another unveiled truth, she passed by the room quickly.

Chapter Eight

After his bath, Courtney stayed with Cameron until he fell asleep. Then, when she was certain that he wouldn't get up again, she headed downstairs. Normally, something in her told her what to do, how to soothe a person when they were overwhelmed, but this time, considering Brett's already misfortunate situation, she was speechless.

Inching past the door, she looked in the den and saw him standing at the window looking out at the moon.

"Brett," she said in a near whisper.

He turned around slowly, his eyes swollen from tears. "I'm embarrassed that you have to see me like this," he said, shaking his head.

Courtney went inside and closed the door. "You don't have to be embarrassed in front of me."

"I just don't know how I could be so stupid. I mean, how could I not see this when it was right in front of my face? I always thought he looked more like her than me, but I never thought that he wasn't mine." Tears ran down his face again.

"He *is* yours," Courtney said, walking up to him. Carefully, she put her hands on his back.

"You're the only thing that he's ever known, and you're the only one that he's got."

Brett swallowed hard. "What was so wrong with me that she couldn't just love me?" he asked angrily as he turned and looked at her. His icy blue eyes burned through to her core.

Courtney's heart broke for him. "Some people never love anyone but themselves. It's not your fault. You tried to be a good husband and a good father." She took his large hand and threaded it through her own. "Come sit down. And I'll go and fix you some tea. It will calm you down and allow you to rest. You have to get up early in the morning and it's getting late."

With a blank stare, he followed her to the sofa and sat down. Courtney looked around the room and bit her lip. While the place was nice for sitting and reading or watching television, it was not a bedroom. And in the state that he was in, he really needed to rest comfortably.

"Why don't you sleep in the guest room or in my room, and I'll sleep down here tonight. It may help with your nightmares," she pleaded.

Brett wiped his face and pinched the bridge of his nose. A major headache was looming. "I'll be fine," he said, closing his eyes.

"Are you sure?" she asked concerned.

He shook his head. "Yeah."

She couldn't help but think back to his previous statement. *His life was a comedy of errors.* But why? He was strong, dependable, brave...and misfortunate.

"I'll be right back. I'm going to fix your tea," she said unsure if she should leave him alone.

Brett was too consumed by his thoughts to hear her. With dried tears staining his face, he sat on the end of the sofa staring at the television.

Courtney rushed into the kitchen and quickly put on a kettle. Within minutes, she had fixed him a warm cup of tea and returned to his side.

Kneeling in front of him, she passed him the little white tea cup and brushed a hand over his face. Their gazes locked as her thumb stroked over his flesh.

Brett took the cup thankfully and set it beside him. Too shook up to say a word, he sat brooding and looking at the ground.

Courtney took the remote and turned off the television, then rose up from her position. Smoothing her hands over her jeans, she looked over at the door.

"I'll just leave you here to...think," she said, looking at the crown of his head. "I'm so sorry, Brett." She was lost. What more could she do for him?

Brett slowly looked up at her and nodded. "Thanks," he said solemnly. "I appreciate it." His voice was hard now.

Courtney smiled, then turned and walked out of the door, turning off the light as she left.

In the silence and darkness of the den, Brett pulled off his shirt and jeans and laid down on the couch in his boxer shorts. With one hand cocked up behind him, he looked at the ceiling fan and with the other hand, he ran his thumb over the bottom of his wedding ring. Why did he even have this damn thing on anymore? Snatching it off, he threw it across the room.

He truly felt like acting out - like tearing the walls down around him - but he was drained of even the energy to do that. All he knew was that the boy he had loved since the first day that he had laid eyes on him was not his; the woman he had loved unconditionally was never his, and the life that he had created around him was not real. The most painful part of the equation was that he had been too blind *or too stupid* to notice or suspect anything, which made him feel that he was to blame.

Fool me once, shame on me. Fool me twice, then I must be an fucking retard, he thought to himself.

Cameron crossed his mind - his delicate little features seared into his brain forever. Brett had always thought that the boy had more characte-ristics from Amy's parents, who were both bru-nettes. And while the boy didn't look like him, he had loved him so much until he had never allowed a single thought to cross his mind about Cameron not being his.

Plus, Brett's mother had died suddenly from a heart attack and was not there to tell him her thoughts on the matter. But his mom was always a very kind and tactful woman, unlike Amy.

So unless there was *undeniable* proof that Cameron was not his, she would never said anything anyway.

Conversely, he did love the boy, and there was no doubt about that. And Courtney was right. *All they had was each other now.*

"What kind of woman does this shit?" he asked aloud. The dark room did not respond. It could not. But being left in silence made him angrier by the moment. Hurt started to shield itself with the fuel of revenge. But who could he lash out at? Who was left to carry the burden with him?

Brett snickered to himself when he thought of Amy going down in flames. He imagined her on the plane headed to Japan with her I-pod in her ears, listening to Clint Black and making plans to start a new life with *Jermaine* when suddenly the pilot came over the intercom and told them to kiss their asses goodbye.

He could see her looking around all scared and praying that she would be the only survivor with no thought about Cameron or the family that she left behind. He had even imagined that she might have even prayed to God for his help. But He wouldn't help her.

Reap what you sow and all that.

He knew it was wrong to think in such a way, but he didn't care at the moment. It was the only thought that seemed to soothe him as he began to drift off in troubled sleep.

Closing his eyes, he felt his breaths slow and his mind stop racing. Maybe he would get some rest after all.

***

At exactly two o'clock in the morning, Brett's brilliant blue eyes flashed open with a fright. Sitting up, he wiped his face of the sweat pouring down it and looked around frantically. Another devilish nightmare. This time in his dream, he was in an ambush with his late friend and fallen Marine, Sergeant Allen.

He could even feel the sand and heat on his skin and hear the snap of AK-47 bullets whiz past him as the green chasers continued to fly. The taste of blood was in his mouth from where he had bit down too hard on his lip and his trigger finger was sore from gripping his imaginary weapon.

The mind was a powerful thing, and in his case, sometimes a powerful enemy.

He looked down at his hands, shaking and clammy and slowed his breathing. Wanting a drink, he stood up and wondered out into the dark hall towards the kitchen. He'd sneak a beer before four and drink down a few quarts of water in the morning just to take the edge off. Hopefully, it wouldn't affect the company run later that day.

As he entered the spotless kitchen that smelled of bleach and Pine Sol, he saw Courtney sitting at the table reading her textbook under a small lamp. Pausing, he flipped on the light and looked her way.

"What are you doing up?" he asked gruffly.

Courtney looked up and put down her highlighter. "Couldn't sleep. I figured I'd get some work done." She watched him make his way to the refrigerator. Bending over as he opened it, he looked inside and grabbed a beer.

"I take it the tea didn't help," she said, turning off her lamp.

"Sorry. I didn't even try it," he said, popping the top to a chilled Miller Lite. He took a sip and sluggishly made his way back to the entryway.

Courtney opened her mouth and then quickly closed it shut. She didn't want to pry. Sticking her nose into other people's affairs had been one of her downfalls for many years. It was part of her *Save the World Syndrome.*

Nevertheless, Brett could feel her stare on his back. He turned slowly and titled his head.

"Say it," he said, propping his bare foot up on the wall. He had been around women long enough to know when they had something on their mind. Rubbing a hand down his jaw, he scratched the stubble under his hand.

Courtney closed her book and sighed. "This isn't your fault."

"You sound like that movie, *Good Will Hunting.* Have you seen it?"

Courtney knew his guard was up. "I'm serious."

Brett sighed. "I could tell myself that it isn't my fault, but I'd be lying. And I fucking hate liars." He clenched his jaw tight, and he could tell that his harsh language didn't sit well with her. So, he tried to speak softer for her sake. "You're a good girl, Cort. I don't expect you to understand."

"What is there not to understand? You were betrayed. It must hurt." She looked down at the table. "It must tear you apart, but it always helps to have someone tell you the truth. And the truth is that you're a good, decent man." She looked back up at him, her eyes were full of sincerity. "And it's not your fault."

Brett felt uncomfortable. He put his foot down and looked up at the ceiling. The bottle of beer was clenched in his hand. Shaking his head, he smiled despite himself. "I loved her."

"I know," Courtney said in a soft, loving voice.

"But she was never good to me. Nothing I ever did was good enough."

Courtney thought of her father. "Believe me. I understand."

"Do you?" he asked quickly. He stared at her. "How do *you* understand?"

"My father," she muttered. "He has never been happy with one decision that I have made by myself in my entire life. Just once, I wish he would be proud of me, you know." Her voice trailed off, but she kept her eyes on him even though it was hard to look someone in the eye and admit such a thing.

Brett could see the pain in her eyes, and even in his own sorrow, he felt pity for her. "Who couldn't be proud of you?" he asked sincerely. "Look at you. You're amazing. I knew it the first time I laid eyes on you. Beautiful. Soft. Honest." His voice grew husky. "You're everything a man could ask for and more." His eyes were deadlocked on her own. She couldn't turn away if she wanted to now.

Courtney was unnerved. Her mouth parted in surprise; her heart skipped a beat and butterflies erupted. "It's funny that you can see all of that in me and not see that we have *all of that* in common."

"I don't' know about the beautiful and soft part." Brett smirked and was about to take another sip of his beer but paused. His face hardened. "I have nightmares. I have...flashbacks. It's hard for me to adjust. Being around people in large crowds or being around people that I don't know puts me on edge. Sometimes, I drink too much, and I just want to be alone. That can go on for days...weeks. I assume that my *anti-social* behavior had a lot to do with Amy's growing unhappiness in our relationship. But I couldn't help it," he said deflated. "People expect that just because you swear in, volunteer, and decide to stand a post that you're also supposed to be able to face what the consequences are for doing so without flinching. You're supposed to have this concrete resolution. But no one is ready for what they see over there."

Courtney listened quietly. She could feel his loneliness and vulnerability. "PTSD doesn't go away overnight. In fact, I'm not sure that it ever goes away, but with treatment..."

He interrupted her. "Treatment would end my career, and I've worked too hard to end up on 100% disability with no other skill but killing on my resume. Plus, I'm trying to be a father to a child that isn't mine..."

"Don't say that. Don't ever say that. He *is* yours," she said defensively of Cameron. She frowned and leaned forward in her chair. Her gold necklace gleamed in the dull light. "Where would he be without you? He has no one else. Don't *ever* let him hear you say that. It would kill him." Her eyes watered. "And hasn't he been through enough?"

Brett was moved by her protection over his son, and he knew that she was right. "I just had to say it once. I had to hear myself say it to know it. Just once," he said with tears in his eyes. "I don't want to..." He could feel his mouth quiver. "I don't want to walk around like this didn't happen too. Something has to be real, even if it's really fucked up."

Courtney stood up from her seat and walked over to him. Opening her arms, she felt him grab her tightly and bury his head into her neck. He wouldn't cry. He was too stubborn for that, but he did empty himself emotionally into her.

Her arms wrapped around him. In a soft voice, she whispered, "It's okay. I'm here for you." A sad smile curled her lips.

Brett clenched his eyes tight and held her close to him. The warmth of her body radiated like pure sunlight onto his skin. The fresh, clean smell of her intoxicated him. Swiftly, his sorrow turned into gut-wrenching need.

Brushing his hand through her hair, he looked into her eyes and saw a vulnerability that made him suddenly fiercely possessive. A growl escaped him. Agog, he moved his large hand to her neck. The pulse of her heart pounded through his fingertips. He leaned in and pressed a kiss to her neck first then her chin and finally he kissed her pouty, full lips. Tasting the sweet nectar in her mouth again sent chills down his spine and without intending to, he picked her up and pinned her against the wall.

Courtney kissed back, lost in the moment. She ran her hands over his bulging biceps, amazed at his strength and aggression. She closed her eyes and felt his hands gripping her thighs, making their way up her legs. Her breaths began to quicken, her sex clenched tight.

His thick erection prodded in between her thighs pointing its rigid heat at the core of her.

She was suddenly confused. She wanted this. Oh, she wanted this, but it was too soon. He was vulnerable, not thinking clearly. Things could change for him in the morning when his thoughts were not fogged by more drama. But she would still want him. It would just be another tragedy to go down in the books.

Pulling away from his kiss reluctantly, she pushed her hands against his chest. "Brett," she panted. "We shouldn't."

Brett face was red with heat. Gritting his teeth, his eyes wild with desire, he put his forehead on hers and slid her obediently down the wall. Removing his hands from inside her panties, he looked down at her and licked his wet lips.

"I know," he said, getting his bearings. "But it's just getting so hard to fight."

Courtney was shivering all over. Her satin panties were wet from the silky milk that had already started to glisten between her thighs. She looked down at her feet and couldn't help but notice his magnum-size erection. It only made her want him more.

Brett stepped away. Under heavy, lust filled eyes, he gazed at her, wanted her.

She looked up at him, embarrassed to have stopped him. "I don't want this to be just another mistake that ends up effecting Cameron."

His eye twitched. "I don't want you to wake up and start to see me like Amy did."

"I would never do that," she said in a high pitch.

"And I would never *not* want you. I'll want you tomorrow when I wake up, Cort." He moved closer to her. "I'll want you tomorrow evening when I come home and see you again, next month, the year after." His voice was low and sexy. His eyes telling of his desire. He ran his hands through her hair and watched her eyes grow lazy.

Courtney couldn't catch her breath. His masculinity invaded her. "And I will want the same," she said swallowing hard. "So maybe this isn't a good idea. Maybe I should go."

"Oh, I'm not letting you go," Brett said firmly. He shook his head and pushed against her. "I can't."

Courtney tried to fight him, but the feel of his fingers against her skin betrayed her mind. Flesh began to speak to flesh, and she was no longer in control.

"Brett, this is dangerous," she warned.

"I'm a fucking United States Marine," he answered simply before he picked her up in his arms. "What part of my life isn't dangerous?"

"I want you so badly," she whispered into his mouth.

Brett felt the same for Courtney. His erection was so rock hard until it literally began to hurt. A red-hot gaze of need blinded him. He carried her without a struggle through the house, but they could not make it to the bedroom.

Every kiss became more sensual, every touch became more erotic. He stopped at the steps that led up to the second floor and detoured into the living room. Laying her on the sofa, he snatched her kimono off to reveal soft, pink satin underwear.

His large hands immediately went for her breasts. He couldn't remember how many times he had thought of doing just what he was doing now, touching her, fondling her.

Courtney was half on the sofa, half on the floor, pinned against Brett with her legs wide open. Her hands found their way down his rock-hard chest, past his six-pack abdomen to the curly hair just above his eager manhood. She raked her nails there and made him growl.

He bent to her and bit her pebbled nipple through her bra, then quickly unhooked it to reveal her ripe, ample breasts. The look of her dark, ebony skin only made him harder. In the moonlight, he could see the contrast of their skin. His pale hand over her dark breast. His body in between her dark thighs.

Bending down, he suckled at her hungrily. His tongue was nimble. His hands explored every part of her. He tasted her nipples eagerly, lapping her up as he held her close.

Hot breath hissed against her wet skin, and the sound of him licking and tasting her body made her arch her back.

She gasped aloud. The sensation sent zingers through her body as he softly bit her nipple. Slipping her hand down in between them, she stuck a single digit in between her thighs, releasing a flow of hot liquid as she racked over her clit.

He watched her with pure satisfaction. Snatching her panties off, he lifted her hips in his hands and buried his head between her thighs.

Her head flew back, eyes closed, mouth open. It. Felt. Like. Heaven.

Brett picked her up and flung her legs over his wide shoulders. Kissing her shaved little secret, he opened her more as he kissed her there.

She looked down in sheer agony. The want had grown so in her until her fire could only be put out by one thing.

Lust overtaking her, she grasped his capped shoulders. "Do you have a condom?" she asked, pulling his head up.

Brett rolled his eyes. He was a married man for most of his adult life. There was no use for a condom. Heaving a defeated sigh, he put his head on her abdomen.

"No," he groaned. His words vibrated against her skin.

"I do," she said, biting her lip. "I always keep a couple in my personal things."

"Can we go to your room?" he asked. His blue eyes shimmered in the darkness. A dimple showed in his right jaw.

"Yes, I'd love that," Courtney said, trying to pull her kimono over her.

Now that she had her wits about her, she realized that the last place she wanted to make love to him was in his living room on this very elegant but very uncomfortable sofa.

Brett pulled her hand away as she tried to cover herself. "Leave it off," he ordered. His eyes swept her again. He had to get her upstairs before the mood changed.

Courtney could hear the latex as it slid on his lengthy penis. Turned away from her, Brett stood by the bed in the darkness and groaned while he prepared himself.

It had been years since he had used a condom, though he probably should have never stopped.

While he was busy, Courtney had a chance to better admire all the muscles that made up his back and led down to his narrow waist. It only made her want him more. He looked amazing.

"What's wrong?" she asked, laying in the bed waiting. Her fingers found themselves between her legs again.

He looked back at her quickly and then back down at himself. "This condom is for a little shaver," he said grunting. "I'll have to check and make sure that it doesn't rip during the process."

She bit her lip. "We'll keep an eye on it. Does it hurt you?" She was eager to see what he looked like from the front.

Brett turned to see her lying naked on the bed and felt himself regain the inches he had lost in the struggle. "No, I'll be fine," he said, crawling between her legs.

His thick, heavy member slapped against her mound as he hovered above her. Lovingly, he moved her long hair off her shoulders and pulled it into a makeshift ponytail then he trailed his fingers down her neck.

With an open-mouth kiss against her jugular, he pulled her steaming legs further apart with so much authority that she doubt she would be able to refuse him anything tonight.

Courtney had never been with a Marine. It was a personal no-no of hers from years of being an officer's daughter, but her mind had always wondered what it would be like to ravaged by a true, hard-core, killing machine.

Not to disappoint Courtney's fantasy, Brett was not merciful. His charm diminished with his kiss. Serious and focused, he planted his knees in the firm mattress and slipped the tip of his head inside of her.

Her tightness confirmed his suspicions. She hadn't been with anyone in quite some time. It turned him on more.

The slickness on her labia transferred to his condom. Looking into her eyes while he played with her aching clit, he pushed forward slowly with even and torturous power.

She felt amazing. Slick heat raced up his shaft as he parted her.

Her mouth opened as he entered her. The girth and length of him seemed to go on forever. Letting out a whimper, she felt her swollen tissue expand. By then, she was paralyzed in pleasure. Goosebumps formed and washed over her skin. He kissed her mouth when he was certain that he was in the center of her.

Connected in every way, she wrapped her arms around his neck and her legs around his waist. His masculine scent of sandalwood and aftershave transferred to her skin as she kissed from his mouth to the curve of his neck.

Still, Brett had not moved. Then, he looked down at her. And when he was certain that she was ready, he struck.

Her fragile body felt like it was pushed into the springs of the mattress as he cut through her body with his sex. Holding on for dear life, she felt his elbows planted just above her shoulders. His back arched and he drove into her. Coiling back, he pushed back into her again. Each time, he seemed to go deeper, grow harder, spread her resolve and stretch her body.

Holding on to his wing-like lat muscles, she looked up at the ceiling and bit her lip. Hot kisses passed between them as he moved, exacting his thrusts in a manner that left her eager for more but weak from every blow.

The tattoos on his body in the moonlight made him look like an animal. Blue eyes stared back at her as she felt his hips rotate from side to side then in and out then harder and harder. She screamed out as he hit a spot that made her back arch. Pleasure. It hit again. More pleasure. He hit it again and she shivered all over.

Instinctively, he buried his head into her ample bosom, sucking on her nipples and pumping into her body in a slow then fast rhythm. His butt tightened every time that he thrust. His arms contracted every time that he pulled out of her.

The sound of suction drove her mad. He was so well-endowed until it made sounds of slapping that beat like drums against her body.

Never had anything felt so primitive and yet so right.

She held on tighter when she felt his arm pushing against the mattress to roll them over in the bed.

Now on top of him, he grabbed her quickly by her hips and lifted his hips, picking her up off the mattress.

"Ride me," he demanded in a husky growl, looking down at her flat stomach.

Courtney had spent days out on the beach surfing. So cardio was not a challenge for her but resistance to his body was. Hard muscles formed in her legs as she planted her feet beside him and pushed down.

He hit the mattress with a thud but refused to concede.

Gripping her tighter, he pushed back, spearing his head into her pulsing sex with speed and power. He nearly grinned when he realized that she was testing him. *Didn't she know that he was a grunt?* As such, every challenge was taken seriously, especially one like this.

With her knees beside him, she put her delicate hands on his capped shoulders and threw her head back, arching her back into his mighty thrusts. Releasing her restraint, she began to counter his every movement with her own, taking him physically.   Wet sex slipped from her womb and pooled in between his thighs.

Brett clenched his jaw as he fought the seismic waves of ecstasy that rushed through him. The sight of her coke-bottle body was breathtaking. Even in the dark, he could see every curve, feel the contour of her skin and softness of her touch. But it had been so long since he had been with a woman who enjoyed him until he refused to come early.

Finally breaking a sweat from working so hard, he pulled her closer to him and sucked on her breasts again. One hand on her round buttocks very near to the center, the other on her back pushing her forward, he lifted her again, this time twisting her to the side.

Before she knew what was happening in one quick move like he was grappling, she was on her knees, and he was behind her. Never had she felt so vulnerable, so feminine. She could feel his hot breath against her bare, sweaty skin as he trailed a kiss down her muscular back. Then a hand lifted up and landed on her backside. She bucked unexpectedly, wanting him inside her right then. He moved his hand down in between her legs to her aching sex and slapped her again. The sensation sent her into a frenzy. She opened her legs wider.

"Please, Brett," she begged. Her sex clenched tighter. "Fuck me."

"Do what to you?" he asked, wanting her to say it again. He teased her, running his hand over her slick sex and fondling her, then tasting his finger.

"Fuck me!" she begged again louder.

He watched her as she grabbed the headboard. *Wrong move*, he thought to himself.

"Please," she moaned again, gripping the wood tight with her long fingers.

He moved closer behind her. She could feel his hardness, prodding against her backside. She arched her back as much as she could, wanting to take all of him. Her long hair splayed over her back as she turned and locked her dark, lusty, hazel brown eyes on him. But she was almost frightened by how serious he looked.

His face was like wet marble, a glint of dominance in his etched features. Every muscle in his body bulged tight with want. Sweat ran down his beautiful, tanned face. Her scent was all over him, driving him mad. He pushed up against her buttocks and put his large arms over her.

She had no choice but to look at his sleeve tattoo up close. It seemed very intimidating now. Shadowing her body, he gripped her hands to the headboard with his own. It was then that she noticed his wedding ring was gone. She turned and looked at the wall, bracing herself for his entry.

Locked under him, she felt him check his condom. A warm hand grabbed her by the fold in her tiny waist, then he pushed through her body in one long, devastating stroke.

She tried to run away from his engorged penis. Only, she had nowhere to go. His large legs, strong from years of humping hundreds of miles, were right beside her.

His manhood was buried up to his abdomen in her. *She was trapped.* And it felt unbelievable! She cried out again.

"Brett!" she screamed. "Yes! Yes! Oh God! Yes!"

As he coiled back, he kissed her shoulder and destroyed every thought that she had ever had about a Marine. Speechless and breathless, she took all of him until she began to burn with desire.

The sound of his body slapping against hers began to drive her mad. Hot and tingling, she felt her arms weaken. Sounds of sexual pleasure filled the room. A feminine whimper preceded male dominating moans.

"I've wanted you so bad," he whispered into her ear as he pumped harder. "And now that I have you...I'm never going to let you go."

Thrusting into her, he watched her as she began to submit fully. Her arch began to flatten in her back; her moans turned to cries until she finally realized she was no match for him. He seemed to tear through her without tiring, his force undeniable, his strength unforgiveable.

"That's it," he taunted. "Come for me."

His words destroyed her. She had never imagined he was such an animal. If she weren't already coming, she would have just then.

Brett finally let her arms go, but only to grab her by her long hair. Without inflicting any pain, he took her hair and fisted it.

Pulling her head back to see her beautiful face, he kissed her bruised, open mouth as he felt her sex clench around him, pulse hard and then climax suddenly. Her eyes told on her as they averted to the ceiling and then rolled back in her head.

The Lieutenant Colonel's daughter had arrived. He smirked as he sucked at her bottom lip.

Holding her around her waist, Brett pumped inside of her as she sat on her knees, tears running down her face, silky liquid running down her legs, sweat running down her body. Brown breasts bobbed against the gravity that pulled her down every time his thrusts sent her up in the air.

Familiar sensations started to assail his tense body. His large palm rested at her lower back and pushed her down into the bed. Her face landed on the soft, goose-down pillow. As he let go of her hair, it fell over her shoulders, over her face.

On top of her, holding her waist as tightly as he could with one hand and his other hand on her slender shoulder, pumping into her body with devastating blows, he finally allowed himself to freely release.

The surge of power and hot seed paralyzed him as it shot from his penis into the safety of the condom.

Picking her up by the waist as he came, he held her broken body in his hands. His masculine, virile growl echoed throughout the room, claiming her as he did so.

The mere sound of him made her come again. One last time. This time harder. A final cry escaped her.

Never in her life had she been so thoroughly explored.

Collapsing under him, Courtney felt as though her body had been shattered. She turned and rolled over onto her back, disoriented and dazed.

Brett was still on his knees with one hand against the headboard, the other on his hip. His face was like stone. His breaths calmed quickly. After all, the storm had passed.

Looking up at him in amazement, she heard the alarm go off. It startled her. Lifting up on her elbows, she moved her tousled hair from her face.

4:00 a.m. on dot.

"Time for work," she said hoarsely. It hurt to swallow. She did so slowly.

Brett bent down and sucked her pebbles nipples one last time and kissed her lips again, grateful that she had shared her body with him.

She kissed him back passionately, pushing her exposed breasts against his chest. Her sensitive nipples were still rigid as they grazed him. He reached down and grabbed them in his hands and squeezed them tightly.

It had been too long since he had enjoyed sex this much, and she still looked absolutely amazing, even though her hair was now wild and her body sweating and wet.

His hands roamed her body, feeling the slickness in between her thighs that had pooled on the mattress below them.

There was no way in hell he was leaving this bedroom without getting his share. Reaching over to hit the alarm, he opened her legs again.

"I've got a few more minutes," he said with another condom in his hand.

Courtney was speechless but ready. "God Bless the Marine Corps," she said, biting her lip.

Chapter Nine

It had only been a few weeks, but Brett Black felt like a new man. There was no more Amy and no more worry. Just work and play. He could barely get home in the evenings. He could barely leave for work in the morning. Even Cameron seemed to be doing better.

As the alarm went off for a new day to begin, Brett reached his free hand over and hit the dial, then returned to Courtney's warm embrace.

She rustled awake under him, running her hands over his bare chest as she stretched out.

"Baby, get up," she said, rolling over.

Brett grabbed her quickly. Running a hand over her naked backside, he pulled her to him. "I don't want to get up. It's too fucking early," he groaned into her ear. "Let's just lay here for a minute."

Courtney smiled. "You were almost late a few days ago. No, you have to get up," she said, trying to pull away from him. It was hard for her too. Her heart ached every time that he left the house. And while she spent her days busy with studying, online classes and taking care of Cameron in the afternoons, she could barely wait for the end of the day.

Brett was getting ready for a few days out in the field and the thought annoyed him, but he tried to keep it pushed in the back of his mind. He didn't know how he would deal with being away from his family that long. *His family.* Now, that was a comforting thought. For the first time in his life, outside of the Marine Corps, he felt like he belonged to something special.

"Get up," Courtney said again.

"Alright," Brett finally said yawning. Pulling himself from the bed, he stood up naked and stretched. He watched her loving gaze travel the length of him. Instantly, he got hard. He bent to her and kissed her forehead.

"You got ten minutes?" he asked, putting his hand on her hip.

"Five," she said, looking at the clock.

"Seven," he bargained as he crawled in between her legs.

"Okay, ten," she said as she felt him enter her. *Ten glorious minutes.*

***

At five o'clock on the dot, before the sun could rise, Captain David Lawless stepped out of his oriental blue 325i BMW in his perfect desert uniform and cover and looked around his new home.

Camp Lejeune. The place grunts came to become great after a short stint at the SOI, preceded by Parris Island. No matter whether you were a woman or a man it was balls to the wall here. You either grew some or shipped out.

He loved the smell of the thousands of pine trees, the heat that evaporated any coolness in the air, the sound of Marines training even when the black flag hung as a warning on the pole, the sight of morning runs that went for miles in the rain, shine, sleet or snow. Hell, USPS got their motto from them, because Recon *always* delivered. Nothing about this place was soft. There were no flowers planted, no picnics by the beach. There was only training, and he was ready to get some.

As he stepped into the company office a solid six feet three, two hundred and fourteen pounds of hard-core grunt, his father was waiting with a proud smile.

David dropped his bags and saluted his father out of sincere respect, even though one did not normally salute inside a building.

This was a proud moment for the Lawless men. David had been subjected for years to rough, unrelenting training because of his last name and his father's reputation. His mentors and superiors alike had been tough on him both in the classroom and the field, put him through more than the others, and made him work hard to earn the rank of Captain. In short, he had gone through hell to arrive at his father's footsteps.

"Captain David Lawless reporting for duty, sir," he said with a stone face and deep, brooding baritone. Not a stitch was out of place on the coffee-colored Marine. His hair cut was perfect; his uniform was perfect; his stance was perfect, and his reputation was flawless.

"At ease, Captain," Lieutenant Colonel Lawless said as he watched his son move to parade rest. "You look...good," he noted, looking his boy over. "Hope Pendleton didn't make you soft though."

"No, sir," David answered. "There is no room for soft in the two-five, sir."

"Are you ready to serve the men of Bravo Company, oversee their training, lead them to battle, stand by them, die if necessary to accomplish any mission that Marine Corps via the Second Reconnaissance Battalion hands down to you?" the colonel asked sternly. His neck stuck out as he spoke, and he rose up on is tiptoes to tower over his son.

"Yes, sir," David answered with conviction. Unflinching, he stared straight forward.

"Good. Just because you are my *seed* doesn't mean that you'll receive any slack. In fact, nepotism is not looked upon favorably, so you can just about imagine that I want things to be so close to perfect the only person who would know it's not perfect is Jesus Christ himself. I expect the best from you at all times. I expect you to be honest, fair and just with each of these men. I expect you to put them first and your own needs last. I expect the best. There is no room for anything less in Recon."

"Yes, sir."

The colonel tried not to crack a smile. His raspy voice lightened. "I also expect you to meet your mother and me for dinner tonight at seven. She hasn't seen your face yet and is about to drive me to Four Alpha of the naval hospital."

David smiled. "I'll be there at 6:45, sir," he answered with his chest stuck out.

"Good. Well, carry on, Captain. I'll have my eye on you," the colonel said as he left him in the care of his new company. "Semper Fi."

"Semper Fi," David answered.

***

Brett pulled up to the battalion office and parked his car. Wolfing down the last of his protein bar, he jumped out and headed inside, slipping on his cover before he entered. As he crossed the threshold of the office, he got a funny feeling in his gut. Throwing his wrapper in the garbage can, he looked around suspiciously and stopped at the company First Sergeant's desk.

"What's up, First Sergeant?" he asked, looking at the company commander's closed door. "Has the new guy arrived, yet?" The conversation lingered on informal but still could pass the grade.

"He's in there," First Sergeant said, sipping on his coffee. He never bothered to look up from his cell phone. Moving his thumb slowly, he chuckled and returned a text.

"Who is it?" Brett asked, trying to pull the man's attention from his phone.

"David Lawless. Colonel Lawless's *clone*. Looks just like him. Speaks just like him. Probably thinks just like him. But I think he's going to be alright. He seems to know his shit. Might be a little *moto* at first though." *Moto* was the grunts' way of identifying people who were excessively motivated about their jobs, and it was no compliment.

"So, he's not a boot?" Brett asked.

"Nope. Like I said, he knows his shit, Staff Sergeant." First Sergeant turned his back to Brett and started to text his wife again. If he had not been preoccupied, he would have surely seen Brett go pale.

What kind of shit storm was he headed into now? He had managed to stay under the radar so far, but with another one of Courtney's family members so close, he was bound to be found out sooner or later.

Courtney had told him that she hadn't told her father his last name or the unit that he belonged to, but the entire situation still made him uneasy. Plus, now that they were in a serious relationship, sleeping together *every single night* and living together in his house, when her family did find out, they would swear that was his primary intention anyway.

The company commander's door swung open and Lawless stepped out with a clipboard in his hand and scowl on his face. "Morning, Staff Sergeant Black," Lawless said, reading Brett's name tape.

Brett turned towards him and sized him up. "Morning, sir."

Captain Lawless walked up to him and did the same. He had read Black's file. He was an impeccable Marine and up for promotion soon, if he played his cards right, considering he was already a *Gunny-select*. He was an excellent marksman, a great man in the field, a decorated OEF and OIF vet and seemed to be made of the right kind of stuff to lead his unit.

Evidently, the Staff Sergeant had lost some Marines in his last tour but had managed to save several by calling in an airstrike during an ambush up in the hills of Afghanistan.

He also had read that Black was one of the Marines who had recently lost his wife in that incredible plane crash and was taking care of a child by himself. He found that commendable.

"Muster for accountability at 5:45 before PT," Lawless said to the First Sergeant as he looked down at his watch.

"Yes, sir," First Sergeant said, finally putting away his cell. He stood up behind his desk, looked over at Brett and walked away. Like he said, the guy was *moto*.

***

After a long day at the base with the new company officer, Brett could barely make it to the truck. Throwing his gear in the back as the heat beat down on him, he jumped up in the truck, slammed the door and headed out.

Removing his cover, he didn't even have to look to know that he had that horrible tan around the rim again. Blasting the air, he turned on his radio, hit song 3 on his Kung-Foo Fighters CD and floored it out of Camp Lejeune.

Taking a detour to a local Jacksonville bar that he often frequented, he met Joe for a quick drink. It had been a while and when Joe saw him actually walk inside, he raised his beer and laughed.

"I didn't think you would make it," Joe said, passing him a beer.

"Hell, I didn't think I was going to make it either," Brett said, sitting down on the stool beside Joe. The chilled beer felt good against his skin, but he knew that it would feel even better going down his throat. He downed it quickly and ordered another.

"So Alpha Company got Baby Lawless, huh?" Joe said, turning back around to face the television playing the game in front of them. "Damn, I'm glad to be in Bravo Company now."

"Baby Lawless?" Joe smirked. He had never heard the nickname but it fit. "This guy had us do a ten-mile run today and then hit the fire range. I thought we were going to be there all day. Then all of a sudden, he looks at his watch, wraps things up and bows out. Hopefully, he has a wife or a girlfriend or something that was as demanding as Amy. Because ugh..." He couldn't even finish his sentence he was so tired.

"A *get-your-ass-home* type," Joe said, shaking his head. "You could never get that lucky. So where in the hell have you been, man? The whole purpose of you getting some help at the house was so that you could actually spend some time outside of it."

Brett took another sip of his beer and turned to Joe. Lowering his voice, he squinted his eyes. "How long have we been friends?"

Joe shrugged his shoulders. "Shit. Years."

"So, I need you to keep something between us."

"Name one person that I've ever shared anything with about you?"

"Not even Judy on this one," Brett demanded.

Joe moved in, knowing whatever Brett was about to share would be juicy. "I'm listening. And I won't tell Judy." He wasn't sure if that was a lie or not, yet. It would depend upon the secret.

Brett sighed. "I'm sleeping and living with Colonel Lawless's daughter."

"What happened to the nanny? The Redwood girl from the beach?"

"*Redbrook*," Brett corrected. "They are one in the same."

Joe took a minute to process what Brett had just told him and then ordered another drink as he laughed out loud. "You are severely fucked, my friend. Please tell me that this is just a fling, and no one is going to find out about it."

"I know it's only been a few weeks but..."

"Oh, hell no," Joe said, shaking his head. "Not the L-Word."

Brett nodded. "I love her."

"Have you told her?"

"No," Brett said quickly. "I don't want to run her off."

"Does her family know that a white, enlisted grunt is screwing the shit out of her?" If the woman in question had been anyone else, Joe might have laughed. Instead, he narrowed his gaze on his best friend. This *was* serious.

"No one knows," Brett answered again.

"Can't keep it a secret forever," Joe warned. "Lejeune may be big, but it's not that big."

"I know." Brett looked down at the bar. "I know."

***

By the time that Brett got home, Courtney and Cameron were fully dressed and about to walk out of the door. As he came into the living room, she greeted him with a kiss on his full mouth that took a few minutes to finish, and then pulled away.

"We're going to my parents' house. And we're running late, so we have to go. I fixed you dinner. It's on the stove, and I left you a little honey-do list."

Brett still had her by the waist. "Your honey-do list is never small."

"Hmm," she smiled. "Do you want to go with us?"

Brett let her go. "No. I don't think that's a good idea." He looked down at his son, who was faithfully ear-hustling. "Go in the den for a minute," he ordered Cameron as he bent and kissed the top of his head.

"Brett, we're going to be late," Courtney said, looking at her watch.

"This will only take a minute." When Cameron was out of sight, he turned to Courtney. "David Lawless is my new commanding officer. I met him today."

Courtney's eyes widened. "Oh shit." Sitting on the couch, she dropped her purse. "I am going to dinner tonight to see him."

Brett sat beside her and rubbed her back. "Baby, this is where we have to begin to tread lightly."

She looked over at him. "What does that mean? Are you ashamed of me?" Hurt laced her gentle voice.

"No," Brett said with conviction. He took her hand. "Baby, I am not ashamed of you at all. If anything..." his voice trailed off. He didn't really want to say what he was about to say either. Instead, he redirected. "I just need some time to ensure that things don't get too out of control at the base. You don't know how grunts are. This is considered a major infraction. I mean," he touched her face, "I have the Colonel's most precious possession in my hands." His voice was soothing.

Courtney couldn't help but smile. "Brett, I have a confession to make. I was holding on to it, because I didn't want to scare you. But now I know you're wondering if all of this is worth it. So, I know I need to tell you."

Brett knew that Courtney never rambled. He watched her carefully. As she curved her mouth to spill her confession, he put his index finger over her pouty lips. "I love you, too."

There was a long silence filled with joy. Brett knew the moment he saw the teary mist in her eyes that she was pleased, and he had not made a mistake or moved too fast.

Leaning in, she kissed his lips again. Only this kiss did not speak to the time or the people waiting on her. This kiss spoke to the need he had met, the void he had filled. Melting into his muscular embrace, she felt him pull her into his lap and run a strong, sturdy hand down her neck to her breast. The beast in him was clawing to be unleashed.

"I love you, Brett Black," she whispered in between the constant sucking of her lips.

Hearing the words for the first time made Brett breathe a little easier. Suddenly being found out by his superior officers and possibly killed on a dirt road somewhere in North Carolina wasn't such a big deal.

Tangled in her kiss, he found his way up her dress and pulled at her underwear.

"Brett," she said, feeling his lips trail down her neck. "I'm already late for dinner." She swallowed hard as her mouth watered. She wanted him inside of her now. There was no denying that.

"Let them wait," he said in a husky tone. He acted before she could change her mind.

Picking her up, he quickly whisked her up the staircase and into the bedroom. Kicking the door shut behind him, he threw her on the bed and pushed up her dress. His mouth watered. "Since I don't get dinner with the rest of you, I think I'll grab a bite to eat right now," he said in a deep southern baritone.

"A good thing the kitchen's open," she said seductively as she raised her hips and pulled her panties down her stellar thighs. "Try not to make a mess of me," she said, throwing her panties at him.

Quickly, he caught them in his hand. "No promises."

Her hair had fallen out of its bun and fanned across the bed just the way that he liked.

She watched him peel out of his jeans and t-shirt to reveal his perfect body. His thick erection stood tall, throbbing and aching for release. Anxiously, he grabbed a condom and slipped it on then dove into bed on top of her. The hard column of his penis slid over her belly then down to her opening. Trailing a kiss over her lips, he looked into her eyes.

"Ten minutes," she whispered in his ear.

"Fuck that. You'll be done when I'm done with you," he growled in her ear.

His words numbed her resolution. She moved his bulging head to her heated center and opened her legs wider. Pushing her belly against his, she parted her mouth for another kiss but when she looked up, he moved down between her legs.

Crying out, she clawed the sheets as she felt his tongue feather over her mound. A tingling sensation ripped through her senses and made her arch her back. He quickly pushed her back down with his palm and yanked her legs toward him.

***

The family was right in the middle of desert when Courtney came through the dining room entryway with Cameron holding her hand. The colonel and his son were the first ones to turn and look at her.

"I'm here," she said with a bright, glowing smile.

"You're late," the colonel said, looking at his watch. He felt his wife look at him. He quickly changed his tune. "But at least you made it. Who is this with you?"

"This is Cameron," Courtney said, setting down her bags and taking Cameron to the chair beside her mother. It was about the only place he'd be safe in this house.

"Hi, Grandma Lawless," Cameron said happily.

Diane rubbed his rosy cheeks. "How are you, Cameron?"

"Fine," he answered with a smile.

"It seems we are the only ones who don't know the little fellow," Colonel Lawless said as he wiped his mouth with a white linen napkin. He sat his large elbows on the table, ignoring Diane's growing irritation with his table manners.

"He's my employer's son," Courtney said, walking over to her brother. "Hey Davy," she said, kissing his cheek.

"Hey, Sis," David said, hugging her tight. "You look great."

"She's glowing," the colonel said, noting his daughter sunnier than normal disposition. He immediately became suspicious.

Courtney ignored her father and took a seat beside her brother.

"Courtney has taken a job with a local, white enlisted man as his live-in nanny," the colonel told his son with a raised brow.

"He's not local. He's from Texas originally," Courtney corrected.

David looked over at Courtney. "Really, sis? A nanny?"

"It's a good paying job. I'm finishing school because of it," Courtney snapped back.

"Still, you're a nanny," David protested.

"Exactly," the colonel chimed in, happy that his only ally in family matters was here to help argue his position.

Diane put down her fork. "Courtney, think nothing of it," she said, waving off her husband and son's remarks. "Your father was enlisted a long time ago. The Marine Corps paid for him to go to school. Then, he transferred over to being an officer right after his short stint in Nam. That is where he gets the title of being a *mustang*. Isn't that right, dear?" she said, sipping her wine.

"I'm proud of how I came to be what I am," the colonel said, feeling her powerful maternal energy from across the room.

Diane continued. "And David, you were accepted to Annapolis."

"I was," David said, turning to his mother. He knew that she was about to make some huge point that would cause both of them to eat their words. He mentally prepared himself to be torn a new asshole.

"So, you see, my sweet and ambitious little daughter, you are the only Lawless who has been forced to pay for your own education," Diane finished as she stood up. "Now, if you'll excuse me, I'm going to go and get desert. Courtney, will you help me?"

"Yes ma'am," Courtney said, standing up from the table with a snicker. She left them alone to *chew on that*. It would serve them right if she read them both the riot act right before she told them what Brett had just done to her for *an hour* before she arrived. It would surely give her father a heart attack and her brother an aneurism.

The colonel watched Cameron eating his food and smiled. "Hey little man. Do you want to be a Marine when you grow up like your father?"

"Yes," Cameron answered with a smile.

"That's good. Hey, what's your father's last name? I might know him?" the colonel said with a deviant grin.

"His name is...daddy," Cameron answered with a grin.

Courtney walked back into the room and snapped her fingers. "Cameron, come in here with me and Grandma Lawless," she said, shaking her head at her father. "You two just won't quit, will you? It's ridiculous."

"If it's so ridiculous, then why won't you tell us his name?" David asked, jokingly.

"Full name, rank and unit," Colonel added with a grin.

"I'm not telling you anything," Courtney said a little lighter-hearted when she saw them smile.

"I guess we'll have to look for someone who looks like Cameron," David said, under his breath.

"Don't forget to take a picture of him with your phone then before you leave," the colonel replied.

The colonel and David had to laugh. So did Courtney. If they were going to find Brett based on Cameron's looks, then they were going on one hell of a witch hunt.

Suddenly, because of Mrs. Lawless, the tension had gone away as it always did when she put her two cents into a family conversation. However, Courtney wondered would her mother's hold be strong enough when they finally did know who Cameron's father was.

A thought crossed her mind and eased her spirit. *He loves me*, she thought to herself as she took Cameron's hand and led him into the kitchen.

Chapter Ten

It felt great to be back on the beach again. Courtney grabbed her purple surf board and headed off into the choppy waves in her yellow swimming suit while Brett laid out the food on the blanket with Cameron.

Soaking up the warm sun on her skin, she waved her hands in the greenish-blue water and pushed out away from the shore. Sound of peaceful bliss filled her mind, and she was no longer in school, in a relationship, a new mother or even a colonel's daughter. She was just Courtney. This was the only place in the world that did that for her, freed her from everything.

Thank God for the ocean.

Back on shore after setting up the picnic area, Brett turned up the radio and rested back on the blanket to get a tan while Cameron built a sand castle with his bucket and tools. *This is the life,* Brett thought to himself as he slipped on his shades.

After a long week with the Corps, he could not think of anything better than spending time with his little family. He couldn't recall once doing anything this fun and relaxing with Amy. She would always complain about it being too hot or not feeling like leaving the house. But Courtney was full of life.

They were always going to the movies, out to eat, to see an exhibit, grilling outside or hitting the beach. And most of the time, she could find things to do without spending a dime.

For the first time in his adult life, he was seeing what other married men referred to as a happy home. It was a shame that he had to wait so long and wait until he was widowed to do it, but he still liked it just the same.

Closing his eyes, he drifted off in a blissful place somewhere in between sleep and a tranquil meditation.

Work had been hard since Baby Lawless arrived. Most nights, Brett had to take a stimulant to stay awake long enough to spend some time with Cameron and Courtney. The only thing he didn't need a stimulant for was sex. His nostrils flared at the thought of it. He raised his head and watched Courtney catch a wave.

Damn, she looked good. She was one hell of a woman and things had gotten even hotter and heavier since he said he loved her. And he did love her, even though they were sort of hiding it.

The thought of losing her made his stomach ache. Where would he be without her? She had swooped in like some comic book hero and basically saved his life and his career. And little

Cameron seemed to be an altogether different kid.

"Wow!   Look at Mommy," Cameron said amazed as he pointed out at the water. He giggled infectiously. "I want to do that, Daddy." His eyes were bright with wonder as he watched Courtney ride in on a large wave.

Brett sat up. "What did you just say?" He took off his shades and planted his large hand into the warm sand under him.

Cameron looked over and blinked. "I want to swim on the surfboard." He had not even realized what he said. He looked innocently up at his father and smiled, waiting for Brett to tell him yes.

"Yeah, well, you're a little too small for surfing right now. But I'll show you how in just a few years." Brett laid his head back down and sighed.

Had his son been around Courtney so much until he thought that she was his new mother? An idea hit him. Lost in his thoughts, he came to the realization that Courtney had become both his and Cameron's entire world. It was the smile in her eyes that had stolen them away. No woman he had ever known before possessed that kind of light inside.

***

Word came from up top that Second Reconnaissance Battalion was on its way back to Afghanistan by Christmas. It was for sure. The news hit Brett like a ton of bricks. Separation anxiety began to immediately set in. He had not left yet and he was already homesick.

The six-week haul to 29 Palms was definitely in his near future, and a serious conversation with Courtney about taking over all of Cameron's parental care was even closer. This was that gray area for Brett. He needed her now in a different way, and his main worry was that *the need* would be misinterpreted as him using her.

During readiness for a deployment, he would never be at home, and she would feel the full burden of their arrangement. He only hoped that the stress of such responsibility would not run her away.

When he first met her, it might have been for the fear of not having a babysitter. But now, he was worried about running her away because he couldn't see his life without her. And without asking, he knew that Cameron could not either. She had become a part of them, and he prayed to God that she knew it.

Training had been going on a month and a half straight since Lawless arrived at Lejeune. And while he had gotten used to the running and the uniform inspections, the ops on the beach late at night and even the long stints in the field,

he could never get used to the thought of going
to Camp Leatherneck in Afghanistan.

The memories from that hellhole made him
raw with emotion and ragged with anger. There
were so many men who had been killed there, so
much work to do. No matter how he looked at it,
what he did for his country was more important
than his private life, because it was his work that
provided his family's safety.

No way in hell he would let those insurgent
bastards gain even an inch against his country.
And no way in hell that his men would ever let
them forget what happened on September 11,
2001.

Thinking about all of the sacrifices and their
contribution to the greater cause made being out
training not so bad for Brett. It had been five
days since he had seen or talked to Courtney or
Cameron. Having spent nearly the last week
burrowed in the bush training, outside of getting
in a shower, the only thing he could think of was
getting back to them.

Stinky and sweaty, he threw his gear in the
back of his truck, flipped off Joe and headed
straight to Swansboro. On the way, he thought
of how many times he had made the same trip
after the same field operation and ended up
arguing with Amy. It made him stop, even with
his uniform on, and dash into Food Lion for

flowers and a bottle of wine. While Amy wasn't worth the risk of being reprimanded for wearing his uniform off base, Courtney was.

By the time that he pulled up to his home, it was nightfall. He parked beside Courtney's truck, grabbed his backpack and made his way in the house. From the outside, there wasn't a light on. He wondered if he should be worried, but his gut didn't wrench. So, he dismissed it.

He unlocked the front door quietly and turned off the alarm. The house smelled of expensive room spray and was illuminated by candles. He stopped at the door, dropped his backpack and pulled off his cover.

"Courtney?" he called out.

"In here," she answered.

He went to the dining room and found her sitting at the table under a candlelit dinner with nothing on but his Charlie uniform shirt and a pair of red, Patton leather stilettos. Her long legs were perched up on the table. Her shirt open. Her hair down. And her lips covered in a clear gloss.

Brett immediately had a hard on. With a crooked smile on his lips, he walked up to the table and sat down the bottle of wine. He carried the grocery store roses over to her. The plastic crackled under the hold of his grasp.

"For you," he said, bending down to kiss her lips. God, he loved those lips.

"Missed you," she said, taking the roses.

"I see." He kissed her again, this time deeper.

She had to pull away for a minute, familiar with how his touch affected her. Her heart pumped hard. "And I fixed dinner." She pointed at the meal waiting for him.

"I see." His hands racked through her thick mane. It fell over on his arm across his tattoo and smelled like fresh roses.

"Wanna eat first?" she asked as her eyes rolled to the back of her head. She rested her head in the palm of his large hand and relished in being in his presence again.

"Not really," he answered, moving her shirt over to expose her perky brown globe. His eye twitched as he bent to kiss her pebbled nipple. His warm mouth enclosed the tip of her. Suckling and kissing her, he pulled at his belt. He managed to speak with a mouthful of breast tangled in around his tongue.

"Where's Cameron?" His quiet eyes moved up to gaze on her own.

"Exhausted. He's been at school, then the beach, then the library. He conked out. Actually, I *conked* him out. I wanted to make sure that he didn't have enough strength after dinner and a bath to stay awake."

Scooping her up in his arms, he headed towards the den. "Well, I don't want to wake him up, considering all that you've done to get him to sleep," he whispered as he tugged at her earlobe with his teeth.

Suddenly, Courtney turned up her nose. "Baby?"

"Hmm?"

"What's that smell?"

Brett had almost forgotten. He bit his lip. "Me. I forgot. Sorry. I need to take a shower," he said, setting her down on her own two feet. He wished at that moment that she didn't have a sense of smell, because he was certain that he could gut it out his own stench. Courtney, however, might gag.

"I can come with you," she said with a naughty grin. "Wash those places that are hard for you to reach?" Her heavy lashed eyes flapped like wings.

Brett shook his head. It sounded good in theory only. "Think about it. Grown men out in the field for five days with an inch of toilet paper and no restrooms, sweating and working for twelve to fourteen hours straight. You sure you want some of that?" Humor laced his deep baritone.

When he said it like that, suddenly Courtney lost some of her enthusiasm. "Okay, I'll wait for you in the den," she said as she strode back over to the dinner table. "And being the good woman that I am, I'll even fix you a plate for after." The candlelight brought out the golden brown of her eyes and the beauty of her flawless skin.

"You may want to eat a little bit yourself, ma'am, to fuel your energy," he said, walking to the stairwell.

The thought of Afghanistan crossed his mind and he knew that after he made love to her, he'd have to break the news. But as she bent to make his plate and he got a view of her perfect backside decorated in only a red thong, he decided that there was no way in hell he would bring it up before. Hurrying quickly up the steps two at a time, he ran into the bathroom to shower.

***

Courtney had never been tied down before, but she had to admit that she liked it when Brett Black did it. It seemed the Staff Sergeant had use for the matching tie that went to his uniform. He had bound her to the leg of the couch and punished her over and over again with his mouth, then his rock-hard body and finally with his eyes as he gazed down at her covered with his seed.

He did right to take her to the den. She had screamed so loud until she had to bury her beautiful face in his chest to muzzle the sound. He had enjoyed every moment of it.

Legs splayed open, heels on, she had bucked hard against his body, taking every inch of him. She had come so hard until she could no longer put together words.

Brett finally untied her when they were done. Her long, shapely arms were limp above her. Attentively and carefully, he tended to her fresh carpet burn made red by the constant friction against the floor. She didn't notice it before, but now she was certain it would leave a mark on her side.

His naked body was glistening with sweat as he stood over her. Breathing hard with his muscles rippling down his marble-like torso, he wiped her off with the throw cover, laid her down on the couch and went to the downstairs bathroom to grab a tube of Neosporin.

Alone in the dark room, Courtney rolled over to her side and struggled to fill her lungs with air. It hurt to swallow from the constant screaming. White dancing spots flashed in her eyes as she squinted to look across the room. Dehydration had set in and all she wanted was balm for her lips and water for her throat.

Running her shaking hands down the leather, she took in a deep breath and smelled him all over her. She inhaled through her mouth and exhaled out of her nose to slow her breathing, but she could still hear her heart beating loudly through her chest.

That was the most intense sex I've ever had, she thought to herself.

Did sex with him only get better? It seemed to. Every time he touched her, he did something new, something more passionate. It kept her wanting more, waiting for the next time.

Even though he was only in the next room, she felt their separation. Love was a strange thing. Suddenly because of it, she was emotionally connected to this man unlike any lover she had ever had before. Her thoughts assailed her with such veracity until she had to simply stop and clear her mind.

Preceded by the echo of heavy footsteps down the hall, Brett walked back into the den and closed the door behind him. He turned on the lamp on the end table and quickly knelt over her. She looked over at him with a lazy smile and watched him rub the salve into her soft flesh, kneading the muscle with the palms of his hands. "I didn't mean to hurt you," he said sincerely as he worked.

His blue eyes washed over her, looking for any other bruises he might have inflicted in his mad sexual rage. Five days was a long time to be away from home. It had shown when he came out of the shower and met her in the den two hours before. He had attacked her mercilessly, left no orifice unattended, no bare skin untouched.

As he recalled his sex session, he licked his lips and reminded himself to brush his teeth.

"You didn't hurt me," Courtney said, opening her lazy eyes. With a smile, she turned to him.

"No. Don't move," he grabbed her waist.

"Baby, I'm fine," she giggled. "I feel...amazing."

Brett's eye twitched. "Well, you most definitely *felt* amazing, but I still should not have been so rough," he said as he sat on the floor beside her. Cocking his legs up, he pushed his back against the couch and scratched his head. "Don't go to sleep, okay," he said, looking back at her.

"Why?"

"I need to talk to you?"

"That doesn't sound good," she said, sitting up. She moved her smooth legs over his shoulders.

Nuzzling the back of his head in between her sticky thighs, he picked up on her feminine scent. His body instantly responded. It already wanted more.

"Down boy," Courtney ordered, looking over into his growing lap. "What's on your big brain, not your little one?" she asked with a huff.

Brett sucked his bottom lip. "We received word today that we are headed to Afghanistan in December, before Christmas."

Courtney's smile disappeared. Running her hand through her long, dark locks she reached out and grabbed his shirt to cover her body. "Afghanistan? For how long?" she asked.

"Seven months." His voice was flat.

"What are we going to do about Cameron? What are we going to do about us? I mean, my goodness." She moved her legs from around him and scooted off the couch. Standing up in her heels with his shirt wrapped securely around her, she looked down at him and waited for an answer.

Brett remembered the many conversations that he had been forced to have with Amy about the same subject. None of the discussions ever ended well. She would always start out with the same questions and end up telling him that she wasn't sure if she could wait for him, if she could do one more tour. Maybe he should have listened to her. He didn't expect tonight's discussion to be any different. It was only a matter of time before Courtney packed her things.

"I just found out today. I didn't want to wait to tell you," he said, looking up at her. Man, she looked beautiful standing in front of him, vulnerable, eager for his every word. He tried to focus, give her his full attention. She deserved at least that. "If you can't deal with this, I understand, Cort. You didn't sign up for deployments and..." his words trailed off. Unable to finish his sentence, he looked down at the floor. Hell, she knew what he meant. He didn't have to explain any further. It was too damned painful anyway.

"That's not what I meant," Courtney corrected. She bent down in front of him and put her long manicured hands on his knees. "Look at me. *Please.*"

He looked up into her hazel eyes lost for words. She reminded him of summers on his family farm, of wheat and the ocean and everything that was good in the world. The thought of losing her crushed him into pieces.

She continued with a slap on his knee. Her tone was more upbeat. "I meant, what are we going to do about our little family...in case? Look Brett, I'm a military brat. Okay. I know what *going on deployment* means. As much as I hate to say it, you could stand the chance of never coming home." Her eyes watered. How could she ever lose him? How could she ever manage to stay apart from him? A strain formed in her throat and her lip quivered.

He wiped her tears quickly. "Five tours so far and I've been lucky."

She rolled her eyes. "You've been blessed. Lucky is finding a parking space. Blessed is surviving a war over and over again." She sniffled. "So the question is what are we going to do? Cameron has become both of our responsibility. And I'm not leaving him or you."

Brett smirked.

"What?" she asked.

His voice was gruff and deep. A dimple exploded in his cheek. "Just something Joe said to me the other day. He said...uh...Marines fall in love in like five seconds and marry in ten minutes. He called us serial husbands."

Courtney grinned. "Well, Marines have a shorter shelf life than normal people. So, they have to move faster," she said, touching his face.

"I don't want to pressure you into anything, but would it be too much for you to think about it? Think about marriage? About marrying me?" He stumbled over his words and cursed under his breath. No one had ever accused him of being eloquent.

"Is that a half-ass proposal, Brett Black?" she asked with a smile.

"Just think about it. Please. I mean, as my spouse I could transfer my GI Bill to you. If I die, you get the house, the life insurance policy, everything I own."

"And Cameron," she added.

Brett licked his lips. "Like I said, you get everything."

"And if you live and you come home in seven months, will I still have you?" she asked with a frown. "Or will your feelings have changed by then?" She couldn't bare it if they did.

"Once I've gotten what I want, will I leave you? Is that your question?"

"Yes," she said, watching his every facial expression.

"What part of 'I love you' don't you understand? I'm more worried about you and Cameron than I am about dying." He clenched his jaw. "I'm not sure that my life would mean much without you two anyway."

"Brett, are you seriously asking me to consider marrying you?"

"I know this comes completely out of left field." He looked up at her. "I know that you're supposed to wait a respectable amount of time, ask the father for your hand...and not already be living with the woman."

Courtney laughed.

"But I'm caught in between a rock and hard place here. I worked so hard to get into Recon. I've always seen myself as a lifer, you know, retiring after twenty-five years. Now, I've got a kid. I'm facing the possibility of being forced out because...well, you know why."

"You know, I could watch Cameron while you were away without you *marrying* me," Courtney said, looking back at him.

"Come on. I've seen how hard you've been working on your degree. You've made my life so much easier since you came here. It's the least I could do."

Courtney chuckled. "To marry me?"

"Well, there are other reasons." He rubbed through her hair.

"Like what?" She smiled.

"Like the fact that I want to come home and see you every night for the rest of my life."

Courtney bit her lip. He was getting better at this *opening up* thing. "And what makes you think that I want to see you every night for the rest of my life?" she asked playfully.

"The grocery store roses, of course."

Courtney laughed. "There is something about the crunchy sound of ten-dollar roses that drives me crazy."

Brett smiled. "Don't knock the roses now."

Courtney felt overwhelmed. Curling into his massive embrace, she pushed up in between his legs and put her head back on his chest. For a half-ass question, he got a half-ass answer, even though she knew he meant well. "I'll think about it," she said with a smile.

Chapter Eleven

Everyone could hear Joe's shriek from across the bar. The eight ball sped across the pool table into the pocket farthest from the corner as he stood up. Putting down the pool cue, he looked over at Brett and shook his head. "You have really fucked up now," he said, grabbing his beer off the corner of the table. "You went and asked the woman to marry you after two and a half months?" He stomped his foot. "I knew it. I knew you were going to do this shit the first time you told me about her."

"How did you know that I was going to ask her, when I didn't even know?" Brett asked, laughing.

"Because you had that sick puppy look in your face," Joe said, taking a sip of his beer. He looked around to make sure no one could hear them.

"I can't explain it. She's just..." he shook his head. "She's amazing. But she did tell me that it was a half ass proposal, so she'd have to think about it."

"No, really. I'm proud of you man. If you had treated her any different, I would have kicked your ass."

"Because she's a sister?" He had heard Joe's *Black Queen* speech a hundred times. So he knew how sensitive the subject was for him.

"You damned right," Joe said, without flinching. "Hey, I may be married to Judy, but I came from the womb of Ms. Earnestine Mabry. You hear me?"

"I hear ya," Brett said, taking his shot.

"So, have you spoken to her father yet?" Joe asked with a grin.

"No."

"When do you plan to do that?"

"After we come back from CAX," Brett answered as the ball went speeding into the hole. He stood up and looked over at Joe. "If she says yes. Hell, she could turn me down."

"Look, you'll be fine. Man up. Tell Ole Man Lawless that you love his daughter, you're going to marry her, and she's going to have a bunch of your little violent ass babies."

That hit a chord with Brett. Scratching his nose with his thumb, he stopped laughing and lowered his voice. "I first found out the first few days after Cort moved in that Cameron wasn't mine through his paperwork from the pediatrician. But then she and I took him out in town and had a test and confirmed it. The test came back like fucking 99.999% that my son is not biologically mine. It messed me up big time. I'm still sort of *not right* in the head. "

Joe stopped smiling. The happiness that he was experiencing before his friend turned to rage. "You know, I was sorry at first that your wife passed, but now..."

"I know," Brett said, sucking his teeth. "Anyway, no one outside of Cort and I know, but you're my best friend...so...whatever." He shrugged his shoulders.

"You're a good man, Brett. A fucking mensch," Joe said sincerely. He hit Brett on the shoulder and sighed. *This guy got a raw deal all the way around*, Joe thought to himself.

"Yeah, well you are too, bro." Brett moved quickly from the subject. He had said enough now. If he never heard another word about it for the rest of his life, he would have heard it way too many times.

***

Diane wiped the tears from her face and hugged her daughter tightly. Courtney had come over after she dropped Cameron off and confessed the entire relationship while she picked out fabric for the new drapes going in her husband's study. She knew that Courtney seemed happier than she'd seen her in her adult life. And now she knew why.

The glow that radiated from her face was like bottled sunshine. And for the first time in a very long time, her daughter seemed to be free.

"I'm so happy for your, baby," Diane said confidently. "Regardless of what you kids decide, I'm just happy that you've found someone who sees how special you are."

"Thanks, Mom. I am too. I just wanted to keep this between us until I decide what I want to do. I mean, I'm flattered that he asked, flattered that he's offered to take care of me even, but I still have a lot to decide. I haven't given him an answer yet."

"I completely understand. Just promise me that once you decide, you'll invite him over for dinner. I don't want him to think that he is not welcome here."

"Don't speak too soon. Dad and David haven't smelled the blood in the water yet," Courtney said, picking up the fabric. "Oh, this plaid has to go, Mom. It's dreadful."

A passing thought stirred concern in Diane. She sat down on the loveseat in the corner and sipped her tea. "You know that I love your father, but he won't be as happy as I am about things."

"Because Brett is enlisted." Courtney shook her head. "Dad is such an elitist."

"Don't be naive, Courtney. I didn't raise you to be *that* blind. It's not *just* that he's enlisted.

Your father won't be happy because of the pure hell he was handed in the Marine Corps simply based on the color of his skin. It wasn't easy, baby. There were so many nights that I just wanted him to quit, just so I didn't have to see him abused like he was. Needless to say that he never did. It wasn't in him. But that was the old days. So much has changed since then. Now, men are judged more equally but racism still exists."

"I know that, and I'm so grateful to him for what he has sacrificed for his country and for us. But still, do Brett and I have to pay for the Marine Corps of Christmas past?" She sat beside her mother. "I love Brett. I do. And at this point in my life, I am not willing to give him or Cameron up for anyone."

Diane smiled. "I wouldn't expect you to, sweetheart."

"I know what is coming down the pipeline, Mom. If I decide to do this, Dad is not going to approve. But I would rather he give him a chance to get to know him before he starts to hate him."

Diane shook her head. "He won't approve, but it's not *his* relationship. It's yours and you have to do what is best for you. That's how change happens – one person at a time."

"Will you please stand beside me on this? I can't do this without you."

"Of course, I will. You leave your father and brother to me. You just focus on Brett and Cameron." She took her daughter's face in her hands and kissed her forehead. "As long as you promise to let me plan the wedding, if there is going to be one."

"Is that all you can think about?" Courtney laughed.

"Your marriage. *My wedding*," Diane said with bright eyes. "Oh, it's going to be beautiful. I can already see it in my mind."

***

Although it was miserable to train in the rain, Brett was grateful for the change in the temperature. The heavy clouds had brought cool air with it and finally relieved some of the sweltering summer heat. Half-way through the day, he actually felt energized because of Courtney's awesome early morning breakfast and their late night lovemaking session the night before.

Pulling his Gortex off, he walked inside the company office and went to the First Sergeant's desk. "I'm going to Subway. Want something?"

"Five dollar meal deal," the First Sergeant said, throwing a ten-dollar bill on the desk. "Tell them to hold the pickles this time."

"Alright. Be back in a few," Brett said, headed back out of the door.

The rain poured down on his face and washed away the grime that had accumulated on his skin. Jumping into his truck, he grabbed his cell. He couldn't wait to talk to Courtney.

Tomorrow, he headed to 29 Palms in the hot desert of California to train for six long weeks. Every moment he had to spend away from her felt like a decade. Calling her phone, he waited patiently for her to pick up but was sorely disappointed. It went straight to voicemail. That hardly ever happened.

It was only a short drive to the Subway on base. And he knew that he would need to hurry if he was going to miss the lunch crowd. Jumping out, he ran out of the rain and into the restaurant without looking up. Shaking the rain off his uniform, he slid in line and sent Courtney a text. *Where are you?*

She texted back. *Where are you?*

Subway, he texted. *I miss you.*

A sweet, familiar voice came from behind him. "I miss you, too."

He turned quickly and smiled. Looking down at her angelic face, he couldn't help but move the delicate strands of hair from her face. "What are you doing here?"

She smiled brightly. "I was at the commissary picking up some things and figured I'd stop here

for lunch. Care to join me?" She pointed over at
her table.

"I'll be right over," he said, scanning the room.

He made his order, paid and took his tray of
food over to sit in the far corner with Courtney
with his back to everyone.

Sipping his water, he looked at her all dressed
up in a soft pink lace top and blue jean skirt with
matching wedge-hill pink sandals and smelling
like his favorite fragrance and felt the sudden
urge to go home.

"Did you put that on to make me go UA?" he
asked playfully.

"No. I just felt like putting on something
nice," she said, unable to take her eyes off of him.
"I can't believe that you're actually going to be
gone for six weeks."

"Me either," he said, suddenly not so hungry.
"Hopefully, it will pass by quick."

"You look so sexy in that uniform." Her gaze
swept over him.

"You like it?" he asked, rubbing his hand over
his chest. He leaned toward her and reached his
hand under the table to rub her leg. "How about
we take a drive over to the beach? It's on the
other side of the base. We could go and curl up
in the back of my truck for thirty minutes or so.
And I could see what color panties you have
under that skirt."

"I'm not wearing any panties, *Staff Sergeant Black*." She licked her lips.

He groaned. "Damn, woman." Sitting back in his seat, he fought an erection. "Six weeks without you is going to literally kill me."

"Well, I have a surprise for you when you get back."

"A surprise, huh." He chuckled. *Now, she was talking.*

Courtney suddenly looked up and dropped her smile. The moment was drained by their new audience. Her face stiffened as she sat up. "David, what are you doing here?" Her gaze averted from Brett to the man behind him.

"I was just about to ask you the same thing," David said, walking up to the table. He looked down at Brett first and then raised his brow. "Staff Sergeant Black," he acknowledged, pulling up a seat. The sound of the chair's legs dragging echoed across the small restaurant and a few onlookers turned to the three curious of why a captain would be sitting with a staff sergeant for lunch.

"Sir," Brett said, sitting back.

"How do you two know each other?" David asked, scanning the room.

"I work for Brett," Courtney answered first. Her eyes narrowed at her brother, urging him to not make a scene.

"So, you're the guy." David turned to Brett. "You didn't mention that." The look on his face was menacing.

Brett's eye twitched. "Was I supposed to mention it?" While he was surely treading on shaky ground, he was no punk. And he wasn't about to be made to look like one, especially in front of Courtney.

Courtney could see that Brett had no intention of backing down to her brother regardless of his rank. She decided to control the conversation as best she could. Breaking a smile, despite her nervousness, she piped up. "I just left Mom. She's doing great. So, I figured I'd come over to the base and take care of a few things, *and* I ran into Brett."

"Really?" David said sarcastically. He kept his eyes on Brett, nearly ignoring her all together. This was a territorial thing for him. "Are you ready to head out tomorrow, Staff Sergeant? Six weeks in the desert training for our soon-to-be deployment is a long time."

"Ready as I'll ever be. I know the drill. I've been to Afghanistan more than most people have been to their momma's house. I guess you could say that I've paid my dues."

"I guess we have that in common as well," David replied.

"Look David, we're trying to have lunch here before he has to go back to work..." Courtney interrupted.

"Don't mind me," David said, turning back to his sister. He was ready to tear her a new one too.

Brett had to bite his tongue and forbid himself from telling the guy to just say whatever was on his mind. They weren't in high school anymore, but he felt the situation had gone nearly elementary. Pushing back from the table, wiped his mouth with the napkin. "Look, if you need to spend some time, speak with your sister, then I can go."

"No, Brett. You don't have to leave," Courtney said, seeing the frustration in his eyes.

"No, he doesn't mind," David said protectively. He shot a dirty look at Brett.

"Oh, I mind, sir. I'm just a *nice kind of guy*," Brett said sarcastically. At this point, he wanted him to say something...anything. He stood up and contemplated just reaching over the table and knocking David off his chair. However, he had to think of Cameron, Courtney and his career in that order. He cracked a smile and looked over at Courtney, who sat watching their conflict unfold with a worried, torn look on her face. "See you tonight, Cort." He knew that statement alone would get David's blood boiling.

Courtney shook her head and snapped out of it. "Okay. I'm going to grab Cameron when I leave here." She blinked hard.

David grinded his teeth together as Brett walked away. He turned to his sister, careful not to make a scene. "Are you screwing him?" he asked under his breath.

Courtney frowned. "Are you serious?" she asked with the snap of her neck. She narrowed her eyes on him. "You've been here ten seconds; now you want to play big brother? Do me a favor and don't try to be Dad, okay."

"He's a fucking grunt, Courtney. You have no idea what you're getting involved in. A ready-made family is not easy."

"I'm a grown woman. I don't need your approval to work for him or do anything else with him." She stood up at the table and realized that she had the entire restaurant as her audience now.

Without another word, she left David at the table alone with their uneaten food. Bursting through the doors, she ran out in the rain and darted in front of Brett's truck as he prepared to pull off.

The water drenched her clothes. With her purse on her arm, she stood in front of his truck with the lights on her as the downpour beat against her body. The outline of her breasts showed through the soft fabric, making her look even more vulnerable.

"Shit," Brett said as he put the truck in park and jumped out of the truck. "What are you doing?" he asked, walking up to Courtney.

Her eyes were bright. "Going with you," she said, reaching for his hand.

Wrapping his arm around her, he quickly escorted her to the passenger side of his truck, out of the rain. Loading her in, he closed the door behind her and pulled off as David walked out of the store to stop her.

Kung-Foo Fighters played on the radio. Rain beat down on the car and thunder rumbled through the sky. It was just the kind of day that would have been relaxing if it weren't for the tension she could cut with a knife. "I'm so sorry," Courtney said, wiping the rain water from her face. She looked over at him with her hands wrapped tight in front of her.

Brett turned on the heat and passed her a towel from the backseat to dry herself off. His gaze lingered on her before he spoke. "What do you have to be sorry about? You're brother's a douche bag. That's not your fault," he said as he turned onto the main thoroughfare. The truck splashed through the large puddles made from the sudden downpour.

"I'm sorry because I shouldn't have put you in that situation." She sighed and sat back in the leather seat as she wiped off.

He huffed in frustration. "Look, I know he's your brother and my commanding officer, but sooner or later, he's going to have to deal with this."

Courtney looked over at him and bit her lip. She knew that he was right. Only, she didn't want him to suffer the consequences of her actions. David had always been an overprotective big brother who would go to the end of the universe for her. And once he got it in his mind that something was supposed to be a certain way, he never backed down.

"Where are we going?" she asked, finally shutting her memory of the many men her family had run off before Brett.

"To the beach," Brett answered. He kept his eyes on the road.

Courtney swallowed hard. "Do you think that we should go now?" After the circus show at Subway, she was not in the mood, and she didn't see how he could be. In fact, she was certain that the only reason he would want to have sex was to get back at her brother for being an asshole.

With one hand on the steering wheel and the other on the arm rest, Brett furrowed his brow and looked over at her. His body was tense and unyielding with animosity.

Courtney couldn't help but feel responsible. After all, it was her family that he was involved with, and that was no easy task. All her life, her father and brother had been over protective and completely unhappy with her choices in men. And normally, they would have been right. But Brett was different. He was the first man that she'd been absolutely proud of. It was a shame that she had to keep him a secret.

She ran her hand over his and tried to calm him, hating to see him this way. "We don't have to go to the beach right now," she said softly. "I don't want to. I just want to be with you."

Easing his foot up off the accelerator, he slowed his driving and his breathing. His square jaw was clenched tight. *Great, now Lawless had ruined this for me today too*, he thought to himself. With his eyes blazing with fury, he looked over at her. "I hate that he thinks that he's better than me just because I'm a grunt," Brett confessed. "What I do in my personal life is not his business."

"You're right about the personal part. But he doesn't think that he's better than you. Trust me. If you were another captain, he would give you the same cold shoulder," she said defensively.

"I doubt that," Brett said quickly. "You don't understand the relationship between enlisted men and officers."

"My brother isn't an elitist. He's just sensitive about me."

"Officers think that they are God's gift to humanity. It's common knowledge. If you were to ask him if his life is more valuable than mine, he wouldn't think twice about answering yes, because to him, it is."

"Okay. I'm lost. Is this about my brother not approving of us, or is this about my brother being an officer?" Courtney asked defensively.

"This is about both. I mean, don't you get it? You're the daughter of an officer. You couldn't possibly be that blind to what is happening here. I'm sure you've heard the stories. We don't mix. Oil and water. Plus, it's against the code of conduct for us to fraternize."

"I'm not an officer. So, it doesn't apply to me. I'm just a normal human being. Just Courtney," she said in a strained voice.

"You keep telling yourself that, and at the same time, we'll keep hiding the fact that we're together," he said snidely.

"I can understand that you're angry, but your view about officers just isn't true."

"And you would know that *how*? You've been catered to on base your entire life. You have no idea what it's like *not* to have that little blue strip on the front of your car to let everyone know that your daddy is the colonel. You were probably born with a fucking salute."

"I don't have the blue strip on the front of my car. I didn't bother to even get it. So, evidently, I don't think that it is that important." Courtney folded her arms in frustration. She had no idea he felt like this about officers. The thought infuriated her, though she couldn't articulate why.

"Go on. Tell me how much of a jerk I'm being," Brett said, realizing that he'd just lashed out at her. However, she didn't have to say anything. He knew that he was being a complete asshole, and he hated himself for it.

"Are we going to make our entire relationship about my father and my brother, or are we going to start making it about us?" she asked, frustrated. She felt like a little rag doll being pulled by both her legs and one arm.

"This has always been about us," Brett said, checking his rearview mirror.

"Are you sure about that?"

"I asked you to marry me, didn't I?" he snapped.

"You asked me to marry you to take care of Cameron so you could go to Afghanistan with a built-in babysitter." Before she could even say the words, she wanted to take them back. Sitting back in the seat, she looked out the window and shook her head. Her voice cracked. "I didn't mean that, Brett."

"You meant it," he replied flatly.

Pulling over to the side of the road quickly, he made a U-turn, digging his tires into the road as he did so. He kept his eyes straight ahead and his lips pursed together. The only sound was that of windshield wipers moving across the window.

Within minutes, he had pulled back up to the Subway parking lot next to her car. He stepped out in the rain and went to her side, opened the door and offered his hand to help her out. The look in his eye destroyed her. She grabbed his large hand and felt it grab and cover hers. Gently, he led her over to her car.

As she opened the door, she turned to him. The rain drenched her again. She wiped her face and spoke. "I'm sorry. I didn't mean it."

Brett suddenly seemed not to feel the rain as it soaked him. His icy blue eyes were pained with the reality of Courtney's statement. Somehow, she suspected that he only wanted to use her. He looked out over the parking lot then back at her as she got inside. "See you tonight when I get home. I'll make sure that I'm not late," he said as he closed the door behind her.

Walking away, he didn't look back.

***

The rain beat down on the battalion office as David waited to be seen. The door to his father's office quickly opened after his meeting and a captain and his subordinate passed David with a nod before he strode inside and closed the door. His father was sitting quietly behind his desk, reading a newspaper and nursing a cigar.

"What brings you in to see me today, Captain?" Colonel Lawless said as he licked his thumb and turned the page.

"I found out who Courtney's employer is," David said, having a seat.

The colonel put down his newspaper and looked over at his son and passed him a shot glass. Opening his desk, he pulled out a ten-year-old scotch and poured him some.

"Who is the lucky gent?" the colonel asked as he set his own glass in front of him.

"Staff Sergeant Black. The guy who lost his wife in the plane crash."

The colonel's eye twitched. He put the cigar in the side of his mouth and pushed back in his seat. A deep sigh escaped him.

"I can see why she was so tight-lipped then."

David shook his head and reached over for the glass. "Salute."

"Salute," the colonel said, picking up his glass and downing the strong drink. He placed the glass in front of him and ran his finger around the rim. "How did you come by this information?"

"I saw them together at Subway...all curled up together like some married couple. Of course, when I came over to speak, they both went straight as a board." He downed his drink and sat up at the end of his chair. "Do you realize how incredibly bad it looks to have a Staff Sergeant in your own company sleeping with your sister?"

The colonel laughed. "You're forgetting that you're in my unit, boy. It looks even worse on my part." He smacked his lips and gave a grin, thinking something in the back of his mind that he wouldn't verbalize. Pointing his long, thick finger at his son, he raised his brow. "You keep your eye on him. Make sure that we aren't being made a mockery out of by this Black until we can figure out where this is going."

"Of course, he would never admit what is really going on over at that house. He's not stupid enough to, but you don't have to be a damned genius to know," David said, growing more and more appalled as he thought about it.

"This is one of those very *sensitive* situations. Black is a good Marine. He's served his country well, and he's suffered a hardship. The Corps would look negatively on any personal business you or I have with him that would affect his ability to perform or function in the workplace."

"I know," David said, shaking his head. His blood boiled but he kept his poise. His father didn't tolerate hot heads.

The colonel shook his head. He wasn't particularly happy about the news himself but it didn't surprise him. This was Courtney that they were talking about. To calm his son's growing agitation, he offered an olive branch. "I bet I know at least one person who knows what is going on over there. I'll talk to your mother tonight, but until I tell you otherwise, keep your hands off of him."

"Yes, sir," David said, standing up. "I better get back. See you for dinner tonight."

Chapter Twelve

The day couldn't have been any longer if more hours had been added. Brett could barely pay attention during inspection. His mind continually raced back to lunch and the short exchange he had with Courtney.

Why would she think that he was just using her? *He loved her for goodness sake.*

Maybe Amy had been right. Maybe he wasn't articulate enough to explain a fart. That is what she used to always say every time he fumbled over his words when he tried to tell her how he really felt. And now, here he was in the same kind of predicament with a different woman, a good woman. Only, he didn't want to mess this up. Courtney was the best thing to ever happen to him, and probably on a hundred other men's radar around town.

The bar was not an option tonight. Tomorrow, he shipped out to the desert across the country. The urgency running through his veins felt like venom killing him with every minute that passed.

As soon as he was dismissed, he made a B-line for his truck and sped home.

When he pulled up to the house, words could not express his relief to see her truck. He ran in out of the rain and closed the front door behind him. Kicking off his boots, he dropped his assault pack and called out for his family.

"Cort?" he said as he headed for the kitchen.

The house was spotless. Not a thing was out of place, and it smelled like her apartment the first night that he had met her - fragrant and happy. He took a deep breath of it and tried to commit it to memory for his long stint away.

Courtney was in the den with Cameron reading him a book. Perched on her lap, his son rested his head back and listened as Courtney read to him and rubbed her fingers through his tousled brown locks. They both looked up at Brett when he walked in, both of them as beautiful as any sunset he'd ever seen. The sight warmed his heart and almost brought tears to his eyes. *How could he lose this*?

"Hey," Brett said, already pleading through his eyes.

"Hey," Courtney said softly.

"Hey, Daddy," Cameron said, without getting up. "We're reading Dr. Seuss."

"*Cat in the Hat*," Brett said, sitting in the chair across from them. "I love that book." He looked over at Courtney and swallowed hard. "Could I talk to you for a minute?"

"Cam, honey, can you go upstairs for a minute while I talk to your daddy?" Courtney asked, picking him up off her lap and placing him firmly on the ground.

"Will you read some more tonight after dinner?" Cameron asked as she planted a kiss on his rosy cheek.

Courtney smiled. "Of course, baby," she said, giving him the book. "Now, put this up in the book box and go play in your room for a while."

Cameron walked over to his father and gave him a hug, then darted out of the room with the book tucked under his arm. When he was gone, Courtney turned to Brett and put her feet under her. "What's up?" she asked gently.

Brett got up out of his seat and came over to the couch where she was. Sitting beside her, he turned to face her and took her hand. Looking down at her fingers, he shook his head. His voice was low and somber. "I don't want to lose you."

Courtney was quiet.

"And I was wrong for shooting off on you today when I was angry with your brother," he confessed.

She raised her brow but did not speak.

He continued even though he suddenly felt desperate. "Cort, I love you." He looked in her eyes.

Courtney could feel herself softening. She took her hands from him and ran them through his blonde high and tight haircut. "Maybe we're moving too fast. I spent the evening thinking, and I've decided, at least for my part in this, that we should slow down. Now that doesn't mean that I don't love you. I do. It just means that I want to make sure that we're making decisions based on that love and not just on circumstances."

"Don't do this," Brett pleaded.

A single tear fell from her bright hazel eyes on to her cheek. She wiped it away quickly. "I'm going to watch Cameron while you're away at CAX. I'm going to stay right here while you're in Afghanistan. And when you come back, you'll be able to make some decisions about your son without worrying about your career."

"This isn't about my career," he said, looking away from her.

"Let's not say any more about it tonight, okay. We've got to get you ready to head to the desert, and I'm sure that Cameron wants to spend some time with you before you go. Plus, I fixed dinner, and I'm sure it's getting cold."

Getting up, she left him sitting on the couch alone with his head buried in his hands. Walking out of the room, she tried to hide the pain that stabbed in her gut. She didn't want to do this. She didn't want to pull herself away from him or Cameron. She loved them both like they were her own, but she also didn't want to end up hurt again.

The entire afternoon after leaving him, she had spent her time wondering if he wasn't being deployed would he even feel like he did about her. Plus, he seemed awfully conflicted about a public relationship. What if there was more to him keeping her a secret than just her father? What if the fact that she was a black woman was too much for him to deal with right now?

It was painful to even consider, but she had to take her head out of the clouds and see things for what they were. This was probably just a relationship of convenience. He could help her with her desire to finish school, and he needed a live-in babysitter. And marriage was just too sacred to barter away just to get ahead.

She wanted a real marriage. She wanted him to get on one knee and propose. She wanted him to confess his undying love for her in front of her family, to be proud to take her into public as his wife and bring her on base and not care who saw them.

Maybe it was too much to ask of Brett, but it was the only way that she would consider marrying him, especially after today. If there was going to be a problem with her father and brother, then she at least wanted it to be about her and her love for a man and not because someone needed a helping hand.

Dizzy with thoughts, she stood in a daze in the hallway leading to the kitchen. Suddenly, she had gone numb. Her mind raced with questions, concerns and confusion.

She didn't even hear Brett when he walked out of the den and saw her standing in the hall. He came up behind her and wrapped his arms around her body. She stood as stiff as a board with tears running down her face.

"Cort," he turned her to him. "This is killing me."

"You?" she said with a sigh. Wiping her face, she cleared her throat. "Look, I'm going to go out for some fresh air. Dinner is on the stove. Don't wait up."

"Please just wait," Brett said, holding her waist. *What words could he say to get her back?* He was disgusted with himself. It was happening again. He was locking up, sending the wrong signals, not saying the right words. And he could see it in her face. He was losing her.

Courtney wiggled out of his embrace. Pointing towards the door, she shook her head. "I'll be back. I just..." She stepped away from him. "I just need to go and clear my head." She shrugged her shoulders and turned and walked away.

Brett stood in the hallway and listened as her footsteps trailed away. Her keys jingled when she picked them up off the coffee table. Then, the front door opened and closed shut.

He slid down the side of the wall and propped his feet up. With his arms over his knees, he sat in a daze, replaying every minute of today.

He knew that this was all his fault. He had been stupid enough to take out his frustrations on her like it was her fault that her brother was his commanding officer and her father was the battalion commander. Hell, he should have been honored, but no, not him.

What he hadn't told her was that he had found out that the man Amy was leaving him for was Captain Jermaine Hodges. That information had come from a good friend in Intel. The mistake he had made was that he hadn't shared with Courtney how inferior it made him feel that he wasn't good enough in Amy's eyes, even though he had willingly gone to face his death for her and her son on several occasions, risked life and limb, saw men blown apart by IEDs, climb the ranks, taken shit and lived in dirt and sand just to make her happy and her life better.

Now, he had allowed his anger for a woman dead and gone to possibly ruin the best thing that had ever happened to him in his entire life. And what had he done about it? Nothing. He had let

Courtney walk out of the door. Amy had walked out of the same door. And he had done nothing about that either.

***

Courtney could barely drive for crying. Wiping her face, she headed into town but wished that it would stop raining so that she could catch a wave and find some peace. The look on Brett's face as she pulled away confused her even more. Why couldn't he just tell her how he really felt? True, he had said he loved her, but what she wanted to know was why. She wanted to be sure that what she felt for him was reciprocated and not just a knee-jerk reaction to his severely fucked-up situation.

This all was driving her crazy. She had never believed in love at first sight before this. But she *had* fallen in love with Brett the minute that she laid eyes on him at the library. And that love had only gotten stronger over the last couple of months.

However, this kind of spontaneous behavior was exactly what her father had been complaining about for years. She always saw the best in people. She always wanted to believe their words, and she would always suffer from their actions. The bleeding heart role was getting old.

"What do you want from me?" she said aloud, hitting the steering wheel.

The painful part was that she was in love with more than just Brett. She loved Cameron, too. She loved how she felt, loved how good it felt to be needed and depended upon.

Most women her age would be out perusing the bars and looking for one-night stands, but she was happy at home with Cameron and Brett. She was happy to plan dinner and teach words and have quiet weekends on the beach and have a family of her own. She was happy with that.

Her phone rang. Swerving as she reached into her purse, she picked it up and saw that it was Brett. She almost put it away but couldn't fight the desire to hear his voice. Flipping it open, she put it to her ear.

"Hello," she said with a sniffle.

"Where are you?" he asked quickly.

"I'm driving to Jacksonville."

"Come back home."

"Brett, it's not *my* home. It's my place of employment, and I'm *just* your girlfriend."

Brett sighed. "Baby, listen to me." His voice was deep and raspy. "I'm sorry for everything that I said or didn't say today. But this is getting out of control. Please, come back *home*. We can talk about it." His southern accent was like silk against her ears.

She closed her eyes but then quickly opened them to pay attention to the road. "I just need to clear my head and figure things out."

"Let me help you. Come home, and we'll talk about it," he pleaded.

"I don't know if this is going to work, Brett. I'm...I'm losing myself. And it took me a long time to get to this point, where I know what I want out of life. Do you know how helpless that feels? To lose yourself?"

"Yes, I know exactly how helpless it feels. And it feels even worse when the person who makes you feel that way is driving away from you." He sat down at the kitchen table with his son and put a napkin in front of Cameron's nightclothes so that he wouldn't mess them up while he was eating his spaghetti. "Everything that you're experiencing, I'm experiencing with you. Now, this *is* your home. We *are* your family. And that is not going to change. So, if you would just come home, we can talk about this...all night if you need to." He listened to the other end of the phone.

Her radio played in the background. Wipers scraped against the windshield.

Courtney finally spoke. "I'll be back in just a little while. I just need some time."

***

It was a little after midnight when Courtney pulled back up to the house. Parking the car, she looked up to see every light in the house was off, and the porch was pitch black.

Climbing out of the car, she grabbed her purse and inched up to the front door with swollen eyes from crying and a hand full of tissue. She was shocked to see Brett sitting in the rocking chair on the porch. He had fallen asleep waiting on her. God only knew how long he had been out there.

As her foot hit the wooden step, he jumped up and took his feet off the table across from him.

"You didn't have to sit out here and ruin your last sensible night's rest, Brett. I told you that I was coming back," Courtney said, feeling even worse now.

"I was afraid that you wouldn't come back," he said, standing up.

Courtney was about to ask why when she thought of Amy. Opening the front door, she motioned for him. "Get in here, now. You've got to go and get some sleep."

He walked in after her. They both were met by an arctic chill. Courtney went over to the thermostat and turned off the air, then dropped her purse at the table. She turned on the lamp and looked across the room to find his eyes as red as hers.

"I didn't mean to hurt you," Courtney said in a low whisper.

"No, I should be the one apologizing. I'm horrible with expressing myself, Cort. I would have guessed that you'd know that about me by now, but you're not a mind reader. I just...have a hard time saying exactly how I feel."

Courtney crossed her arms across her chest. "You seem to express *anger* pretty well."

"Amy was leaving me for a black officer in Japan. An officer that I didn't like was responsible for one of my good friends getting killed in Rahwah a few years back. Amy's parents always hated me for not being an officer. And I guess a part of me always carried a bit of resentment. But it wasn't a big deal until I found out a few weeks ago about who Amy was leaving me for."

"Did it piss you off that he was black? Better yet, are you ashamed of our relationships because I'm black? Is that hard to share with your friends? I mean, I know about Joe, so please don't say that one of your best friends are black, because I think I'll just die here on the spot. I just want to know if this," she rubbed her skin, "is creating a problem for you."

Brett bucked his tired red eyes. *Wow, she was way off base.* "One day, I want my daughter to look just like you. And I'm a fucking Marine. I didn't die for just one color American. And no, it

didn't bother me that Jermaine was black. It
bothered me that Jermaine existed. It bothered
that the insignia on his chest made him better
than me in Amy's eyes. " He stepped closer to
her. "I would never be ashamed of you. Ever. I
may be from Texas, but I'm not...a redneck."

"There are some really good folk in Texas," she
said, thinking of her grampies. Courtney watched his eyes. She knew that he wasn't lying about
any part of what he said, but she needed him to
continue to be brutally honest. "When you asked
me to marry you, *to consider it*, was it about
Cameron?"

Brett paused. The silence between them was
like chaos. He walked all the way up to her and
looked down into her hazel eyes. Swallowing
hard, he took a deep breath. "Forget that I asked
you that time *in that way*. The next time that I
propose, it won't be an offer that highlights the
value-added benefit of college tuition paid and
good dental." He lifted her delicate chin. "The
next time I ask, you won't think it's about my
son. And I will spend every moment until the
next time that I ask proving to you that I love
you, and I'm proud to be with you."

Courtney was lost for words. Now, he didn't
want to marry her? Was that a good or bad
thing? She frowned, lost in the blue eyes and
beautiful face. What had she done? It was okay

to call things off or slow them down when she was the one in control, but the idea of him pulling away was devastating.

"So, you never truly wanted to marry me?" she asked with tears in her eyes.

He took her hand and put it on his chest. "There isn't one part of this that doesn't belong to you." His quiet eyes were clear and focused. Lips pursed together, he breathed in slowly.

Courtney moved into him and rested her head where her hand had been. Listening to his heartbeat against her ear, she wrapped her arms around his back and nuzzled closely into him. She could listen to that sound all night. It was peaceful, powerful and courageous. The hum of it reminded her of how fragile life was and how much he had gone through just to be here at this moment. Tears spilled down her cheek onto his shirt as she stood silently with him.

"I love you and only you," he said, looking down at the top of her head.

Brett trailed his thumb down her neck, lifted her chin up, and softly and sincerely kissed her pouty mouth. It was the softest kiss that he had ever given, ripe with admiration and devotion. Her warm flesh tasted like a sweet elixir to him. He put both hands at the side of her face and pulled her in. Slowly, in a rhythmic, sensual kiss, he washed away her worry.

Chapter Thirteen

Six weeks alone in Brett's house had driven Courtney to the edge. It wasn't that she couldn't wait on him; it was simply that she couldn't take the white walls and boring décor. To add a little spice to things, she had taken some money out of the house account and gone to Lowe's and Pier One, called her mother and did a serious makeover.

Sitting in the living room watching the paint literally dry with her mother as they finished the flower arrangement for the coffee table, Courtney looked around and felt proud. Now this looked more like a place that she would call home. It had taken a few days of hard work and even a little squabbling with her mother about colors, but they had created a masterpiece.

White walls had been replaced with warms colors of beige, sage green and honey brown. And while Courtney wanted to go with a color in the yellow family, her mother had insisted that such an extreme change might unbalance her new boyfriend.

The time with her mother had also given her some much needed clarity. Mrs. Lawless was full of good advice. When Courtney had broken down while hanging the new curtains in the dining room and said that she and Brett had called off the pseudo-engagement, Mrs. Lawless had been the one to explain to her that he only wanted her to be happy. She also assured her that it probably wouldn't be long before he "got it right." To give her daughter a more well-rounded view of the life she had chosen. Mrs. Lawless had also explained the more delicate nature of the Marine Corps and the culture difference between officers and enlisted men.

"It's simply the way it is," Mrs. Lawless had explained in a calm, loving voice that showed her reverence for her husband's profession. "The structure of the Marine Corps has been in place for years, and believe it or not it works. So, don't fight against it or try to make Brett see things differently. The only one who would really suffer from that would be him, and you don't want that. Rather, wait and pray and hope that God will reveal his plan for Brett in the Marine Corps and his personal life. Also, pray for favor for your Brett. Pray that no matter what, he will prevail."

Mrs. Lawless was a gem and as wise as she was beautiful. After talking with her for a few days without her father being around, Courtney renewed her faith in the ability to hold together her relationship and support Brett.

"I think he's going to love the new changes," Courtney said, looking at her watch. The cookies would be almost ready for Cameron in a few minutes.

"Of course he's going to love it. You did it," Diane said, setting the bouquet on the table. "Now, isn't that beautiful? You have a splash of the colors that you love mixed with the calm colors that will make him happy. I use color all around the house to soothe your father, but to this day, he never has figured out why he feels so relaxed when he comes home. It's the colors. I did, however, take a page from your book and make the kitchen yellow. I read in a magazine that yellow boosts the appetite. And when your father lost his after the last trip to Afghanistan when he lost all of those poor men, I had to find a way to make home more warm for him."

Courtney didn't even know that her father had suffered any form of depression. She turned to her mother and titled her head. "Does daddy have PTSD?" she asked quietly as if what they were discussing was a secret.

Mrs. Lawless smiled but Courtney could see the worry in her mother's eyes. She could never admit such a thing publically. It would cost her husband his commission, but she knew that she could trust her daughter. Plus, the insight might help her in her own troubles. "This war has been so difficult on Jeffery. He has lost so many men, some of them friends. Even though he's not there in the field, the burden of his decisions weighs heavily on him." She touched her daughter's hand. "It's weighs on all of them."

"So he does have it?" Courtney said, realizing that she had been so consumed in her life that she had not really gotten to know her father. For a moment, she had a glimpse of herself from the outside and she knew then that she had been selfish.

"He has it," Mrs. Lawless said. "The sleepless nights, the zoning out, the memories. I think as he gets older, it all comes back to haunt him. But I try to encourage a happier lifestyle. I make him go to church on Sundays. It gives him hope and lets him know that he's not alone. And I also hope that he'll retire soon. With your brother here now, it may be easier for him to pass on his legacy and focus on starting a new life with me."

Courtney liked the way that sounded. "A new life," she smiled. "I never thought of retirement as that."

"Well, it's retirement for both of us, sweetheart. Every time your father left on a deployment, a big part of me left with him."

Courtney cringed. "It's driving me crazy that he has to go over there. And you know, he never complains about it. He just talks about making arrangements *just in case*. It must be hard to prepare for the possibility of your death every year. I try to put myself in his shoes, but it's nearly impossible for me. He's so strong and so brave."

Mrs. Lawless knew the feeling. "When your brother told me that he was going to join the Marine Corps, I secretly cried for two weeks."

"Really?" Courtney thought she knew everything about her mother, but in this one conversation she realized that there was so much that she did not know.

"Yes. I thought to myself, *oh I don't want David to put himself in danger.* The thought of losing a son was even scarier than the thought of losing your father. It's overwhelming. Every news report about a casualty, every time someone knocked on the door late at night made me feel like my insides were going to explode. I've lived on pins and needles for...decades."

"How do you do it?"

"They need someone to love them, Courtney. They need *this* when they get back home," Mrs. Lawless said, pointing around the room. "They need to feel that what they are fighting and dying for over there is worth it. And you know, when they are in a fire fight and losing men, rank doesn't matter. They are all over there, bless their souls, being heroes every single day."

Courtney felt proud and depressed all at the same time. It was odd to her that her father's life as a Marine never seemed real until now. This new realization let her know how sheltered she truly had been. Brett was right, she had no idea.

"I have a new appreciation for Daddy, and I'm going to tell him when he gets home," Courtney said with a smile. The timer went off on the oven and sounded throughout the house. "I better get those. I'll be right back."

Cameron came around the corner with toy in his hand and walked up to Mrs. Lawless. Crawling up in her lap, he brushed his little hand over her delicate cheek. "Grandma Lawless, can I come home with you tonight?" he asked, digging in his nose.

Mrs. Lawless removed his hand and reached into her purse for a napkin. "Would you like to come home with me?"

"Yes," he said as she cleaned his tiny little fingers.

"Well, that sounds just lovely. After dinner, why don't you pack a bag, and I'll take you with me. You can swim out in the pool tonight, and we'll watch movies and eat popcorn."

Mrs. Lawless didn't have any grandchildren, but she wanted them. And Cameron filled a special need inside of her now that her own children were gone.

"Is Mommy going to come too?" Cameron asked wide-eyed.

"You'll have to ask her," Mrs. Lawless said in a whisper.

Cameron had been calling Courtney *mommy* more and more. With the absence of his mother and the need for parental protection and love, the bond between the two had come naturally.

A few weeks ago after school, Cameron had asked Courtney if she was his new mommy. It had left her flabbergasted. What did she tell a baby that needed love so badly? Courtney had called her mother straight away and asked her advice. But even Mrs. Lawless couldn't answer as to what was best for her. "Follow your heart," her mother had said. Needless to say that Courtney told him that she would be his mother, if he wanted her to. And so, it had begun. A new relationship was being built, and it was sucking everyone in, including Mrs. Lawless.

"Okay, the cookies are ready," Courtney said, walking back in the living room with the mitten still on her hand. "Who wants some?"

"I do," Cameron said, jumping down off of Mrs. Lawless's lap. "I'm going to Grandma's tonight," he announced as he ran past her knee to the kitchen.

"Again?" Courtney asked with a smile.

"Oh, I enjoy it," Mrs. Lawless said, standing up and smoothing her hands over her skirt. "Since my own children won't give me any grandchildren, then I'll just have to start stealing other people's children."

Courtney shook her head. "Well that gives me a free night. I think I'll hit the beach and catch a few waves after dinner."

"Trust me. You deserve it. You've been giving a hundred percent around this house. I'm sure you're probably a better mother than *you know who* ever was to him. Keep that up and Cameron might start to look like you," Mrs. Lawless joked.

Courtney's smile disappeared. "There is something that I haven't told you yet."

"You're pregnant?" Mrs. Lawless said with her hand over her breast. She said that she wanted grandchildren, but she didn't mean right at the second.

"No," Courtney laughed. She looked back to see if Cameron was in earshot. "It's about Cameron." She walked over to her mother and leaned to her ear. "Brett found out a few days after I moved in that the boy isn't even his. Amy had been lying to him the entire time."

Mrs. Lawless eyes narrowed. *Could this woman get any worse?* "What did Brett say? Whose child is it?"

Courtney shrugged her shoulders. "No one knows. No one may ever know with Amy dead. So, you see..." Courtney checked behind her again and then turned to her mother. "He's as much mine as he is Brett's now."

Mrs. Lawless was moved by her daughter's love. Courtney had always been a giving woman. When she was little, she always brought home stray dogs and cats. Once, she even brought home a homeless woman.

While in college, the only thing that Courtney was committed to was raising money for the women's shelters and had continued with her cause after she had returned to North Carolina. So, it wasn't unusual that her daughter had found another needy family. Courtney always felt strongest when she was needed. It had been her calling.

However, Mrs. Lawless also had drilled into Courtney about her decision. She wanted her to understand how impressionable children were and how hard it would be for Cameron, if she just decided that this new readymade family was too much for her. To walk away from this would be hardest on Cameron, so if Courtney did not want this for sure, she should not lead on that she did.

Courtney had completely understood her mother's concern. However, she just wanted to belong to something. She wanted her own family. She wanted a simple life with a good man, and Cameron had come as a wonderful little bonus.

"I'm very proud of you," Mrs. Lawless said, walking with her out of the living room. "Now, I think I'll have a cookie before dinner as well."

***

The mock operations had finally come to an end and Brett's unit was allowed to leave the desolate desert and scorching sun and heat of the hooch to head back to civilization in the form of Camp Wilson.

After a shower and shave to wash away the stench and sweat, the first thing that he did was use his cell to call Courtney. With his towel wrapped around his waist and the hot water running in the sink, he grabbed his phone and dialed home. He sure wished that she would be there. He hadn't spoken to her in over a week.

With Amy, when he would call home, she would always have an attitude. Something would be broken and needed to be fixed. So, she would start the conversation off by berating him for not being there. Then, she would tell him how hard things were alone taking care of Cameron, followed by the need for money to invest in a hobby that would give her something out of the house to do. He could not recall once when he had called and she was just happy to hear from him.

"Hello," Courtney answered on the first ring.

Brett immediately exhaled. "I don't think there is anything better than the sound of your voice," he crooned.

Courtney giggled. His voice felt like silk against her ears even thousands of miles away. "Well, hello to you too stranger. How have you been?" She ran her fingers through the bath water.

"Miserable. It was 120 degrees today out here. But the good thing is that we're headed home tomorrow. So, it won't be long before I see your face again."

"Promises. Promises." She felt butterflies erupt at the thought of him being back in her arms again.

"How's my son? Put him on the phone. I want to talk to him."

Courtney sighed. "Cameron isn't here. He's spending the night with my mom."

Brett adjusted the phone to his ear. "He's what?"

"Well, he's been going over there a lot since you, David and Dad have been gone." She hoped that he wouldn't be too mad, but she braced herself just in case.

Brett was taken aback but flattered. "She doesn't mind watching him?"

"Are you kidding? She loves to have him over. They eat snacks, watch movies, and swim in the pool. She loves it. And so does he."

"Wow. Okay," Brett said, turning off the faucet. His voice deepened. "So, what are you up to?"

"Well, I went to the beach and hit the waves, and then I went to the library and picked up a few books. Now, I'm here in the tub with a few candles lit, and I'm just relaxing." She giggled. "Did I mention that I was naked?"

"You didn't have to. I heard the bathwater, and I'm getting a hard-on right now just thinking about you." He licked his lips. "Think your mom wouldn't mind watching him again when I get home? I may need a few hours to have a *family reunion*."

Courtney purred. "It's good that you mentioned that. I have a big surprise for you when you come back. Considering that you get a 96 for the Labor Day weekend, I have made plans for us in Wilmington."

"Awesome. I can't wait." She was always full of surprises.

"I can't either," she said softly.

"How's Cameron been since I've been gone? Was it a big adjustment?"

"Well, he's been great. He's doing really well in school. He even picked up a few chores here in the house to make him into a bigger boy, and there's something else." She paused.

"I'm listening."

"He's been calling me Mom," she said carefully. "He asked if it was alright, and I hope that you don't mind, but I told him that it was. I figured I would tell you before you heard him call me that when you got home. I didn't mean to overstep. It's just that..."

Brett quickly interrupted. "Cort, it's fine. Really. I heard him call you mom one day at the beach. I just didn't say anything, because I didn't want it to weird you out."

"Oh, I'm not *weirded out* by it at all. I just...when he asked, I mean when he said it...it sort of became real for me, you know." She breathed in a deep breath.

"I know." He smirked. "He loves you, too."

"I do love him, Brett. This time away has really brought us very close together. And he's such an amazing little boy. When you have to go on deployment, I think that we'll be just fine."

"I'm glad that he has you, Cort. I'm glad I have you for that fact." He missed her even more now. "See you soon, alright." The more he talked to her, the more he became homesick.

"Alright. I love you."

He ran his finger down the fogged up mirror. "I love you," he said sincerely.

***

The gym was nearly empty by the time that Brett made it out of his room. Though he had spent many hours out in the desert working hard, he still had an urge to pump some iron. There was nothing like getting under the bar and releasing all of his frustration one rep at a time. After that, all he would be missing would be a protein shake and a muscle magazine, and he'd be right at home.

Pushing the door open, he swept the room to see what equipment was available and as he did so landed his eyes right on Captain David Lawless.

"Going to be one of those kinds of nights," Brett said aloud as he made his way over beside him to the weight bench.

David was doing free weights with his head phones on, but still nodded his way.

The two had worked silently out in the field for six weeks, putting the objective first as they both had been taught, but even then Brett could feel the looks. David Lawless was not happy about him screwing his little sister. And truly, Brett could sympathize. While he was an only child, he could imagine how something so sensitive might be a sore point. Still, it was Courtney's decision, and he didn't feel as though he owed her brother anything.

David dropped the weights and wiped his face off with the towel. Looking over Brett's way, he cracked a smile. "Glad to be going home, Staff Sergeant?" There was a menacing look in his twitching eye as he talked.

"Yeah, you?" Brett said as he rested back on the bench.

"I'm indifferent. I haven't found that *special someone,* yet. What about yourself? Since your wife passed, have you moved on?"

Brett sat up and looked up at David. "Yeah, I've moved on."

"With my sister?" his gaze narrowed.

Brett smirked and rolled his eyes. "Look, sir, I had no idea that she was even a Lawless until *after* I hired her. She was using her mother's maiden name."

David could believe that. He walked over to Brett and sat down on the bench across from him. "Courtney is special. She's got one of those bleeding hearts and a track record for picking the wrong kind of man. So, what I'm saying to you is this...if you break her heart, if you..." he shook his head, "make a mockery of this family, I'll forget that I'm a captain and you're a staff sergeant, and you and I are going to dance."

Brett could respect that. "I love her. Not that I owe you an explanation, but I can tell you that I would never do anything to hurt her, *sir.*"

"How many times have I heard that before?" David frowned. "Have you ever given any thought to what you're doing?"

"What am I doing?"

"Are you paying her?"

He was not about to get cornered in a conversation where he was accused of slavery. "Of course, I'm *paying* her. She doesn't work for free," he said defensively. What kind of man did he think he was?

David smirked. "What do you call a woman that you sleep with and pay?"

Brett clenched his jaw but didn't answer. He had to try to remember that he was addressing a superior officer in a military installation. Otherwise, he would have already attacked.

David moved in closer, completely unmoved by Brett's growing irritation. "Don't make my sister a whore just because you like pussy," he said in stern low voice.

Brett's eye twitched again. "First of all, if I wanted *pussy*, I could get it any day, at any time. Any bar in Jacksonville has it lined up on the wall like bottles of beer. Secondly, I wouldn't even put the word *whore* in the same conversation with Courtney. And I'm paying her for helping me with my son, not for our relationship." His face turned red.

"If you love her so much, then why won't you make an honest woman out of her? Or are you above that with her?"

"If you're asking me if I'm a fucking bigot, the answer is hell no. And our relationship really isn't your business, is it?"

Mockingly, Captain Lawless smacked his lips and his over exaggerated the consonants in Brett's name. "I'll make it *my business* if you break her heart, Staff Sergeant Black."

"I get it. You love your sister. You don't want to see her hurt. I can respect that. But like I said, what I do in my personal life is my business. I don't owe you shit. And I've paid my dues in the Corps, worked my ass off, stood the post, defended my country and not left a motherfucker behind. So, kissing your ass isn't an option for me. You wanted the truth. Well, I just gave it to you."

"I wouldn't give a damn if you were given the Medal of Honor and the President of the United States flew here on Air Force One to personally hand it to you tonight in this gym, it wouldn't give you the right to fuck my sister. I've said what I needed to say, Black. If you do Courtney wrong, I'll see to it that you never see Gunnery Sergeant and more than that, I'll kick your ass all over Camp Lejeune. I don't care if it costs me my commission. You won't smear my family name."

"Is that a threat?" Brett asked.

"That's a fucking, blood covenant promise that you can take that to the bank every day of the week and twice on Sunday," David said, standing up.

Brett watched David walk out of the gym before he noticed that the few men standing around had heard the entire conversation. They whispered to one another and laughed, making him angrier.

Most men in that situation would have probably felt proud. *The little staff sergeant was sticking it to his superior command by sleeping with their family*, but it only outraged Brett. It wasn't like that at all. He loved her. And he would do anything for her, including taking shit from her overbearing brother.

Glancing around, he felt the heat in his blood boiling over. "What the fuck are you guys looking at?" he asked as he rested back on the bench and grabbed the bar.

He gripped the silver beam and growled as he pushed the weight up, taking his frustration out as he counted out the reps to himself.

Chapter Fourteen

The harsh summer weather had begun to wind down in North Carolina on the first day of September. As Brett loaded into his truck after formation, he actually took a minute and looked around Camp Lejeune as if he was seeing it for the first time. He wanted to pinch himself.

Was life supposed to be this good? Sure, there were some speed bumps like the constant dirty looks he got from Captain Lawless and the now wide-spread and very true rumor that he was dating the colonel's daughter, but aside from the petty things, he was actually the happiest that he had ever been.

The drive home was pleasant with even a faint, merciful breeze in the air. The cloudless day had turned into a peaceful evening, and in the distance the last of a beautiful, golden sun set on the horizon.

He drove with the windows down and his favorite CD, the Kong-Foo Fighters playing, but his thoughts were already in Swansboro with two people who were waiting for him to return from a 6-week training that had trained him dry. Anxious energy made him want to put his foot to the pedal, and rev up his Hemi, but a ticket would only slow him down further. So he paced himself even as torturous as it was.

When he finally pulled into the driveway of his home and saw Courtney's truck, he felt butterflies erupt. It totally took him by surprise to have this feeling considering that it had not happened since high school.

He also noticed that the yard had a new garden of flowers out front were a patch of rugged bushes had once been. Colorful hanging plants lined the entire porch and alongside of his American flag hanging on the side of the house, there was also now a red Marine Corps flag.

And the ultimate touch was the flower stickers on the mailbox around the name *Black*. These were the things that only a woman could add, and while they were small it made his house look dramatically different – like the people who lived here weren't miserable.

Getting out of his truck, he left his gear in the cab and nearly ran to the door. When his boot hit the bottom step of his porch, the front door flew open and Cameron came out running.

"Daddy! Daddy!" Cameron exclaimed as he leaped from the top step into his father's arms.

"Hey, big guy," Brett said, catching him. He kissed his fat cheeks and looked into his brown eyes. "Wow, you have grown, huh?" he said, looking back at Courtney gratefully. His son looked well, smelled clean and appeared happy. *What more could a father ask for?*

"I *did* grow, Daddy," Cameron said, wrapping his arms around Brett's neck. "We cooked for you, too. Mommy even bought a cake."

The sound of his son calling Courtney his mother warmed his heart. "Did you?" he asked, walking up the steps.

Courtney stepped out of the house in a yellow sundress that made her look like spring. The sight of her nearly took his breath away. She was almost iridescent, she was glowing so bright. Her hazel eyes gleamed at him as she reached up and caught his face in his delicate hands. He leaned down and kissed her, slow and passionately while holding Cameron in his arms.

"God, I missed you," he said, rubbing his hand through her hair. She had worn it down for him in long flowing locks, just like he liked it. And it smelled as fragrant as the new garden and as soft as cotton. He wanted her right then but tried to keep his wits about himself.

"I missed you too," she said, pulling his hand to her. Her eyes flashed open from the kiss and her smile widened to reveal perfect white teeth. "Come on. We fixed dinner for your welcome-home party."

Walking into the house, he instantly recognized all the changes that had been made inside

as well.   It looked like the magazines that she
kept in the master bathroom. The walls had been
painted, new pictures hung, designer pillows
were on the couches, new flower arrangements
were on the tables, new rugs on the floor. He
wasn't sure if he should take his shoes off and
leave them in the hallway. Everything just looked
so perfect.

"Wow..." he said, looking around. "You did all
of this?"   He was impressed with the complete
overhaul. It was well overdue.

"You like it?" she asked with her hands
clasped together.   Her eyes were bright with
excitement. She couldn't have been happier if she
had won a million dollars.

"Of course I like it. It looks...like a *home*," he
said with a chuckle. It vaguely reminded him of
being back in Texas. His mother had put great
effort into their little ranch-style home. It was
full of trinkets and photos of their long family
line. Though, he had never experienced that
same type of homey-feel when he moved in with
Amy, he remembered it now and was grateful for
it.

"I used a little money from the account..." she
started to explain.

Brett put his finger over her pouty mouth. "I
like it," he said quietly, looking down at her. He

didn't care how much it cost. It was special because she had done it for him.

Amy had never worked to make their house a home. The walls were white, the wall space was empty and the furniture was basic except for the sofa that had been left to him by his mother when she passed. There was little to no effort in their house before, just a few nice things thrown together. Now, he actually had an idea to invite Joe and Judy over for dinner.

Courtney continued with even more enthusiasm. "Mom helped. She actually picked the colors for the walls."

"It's perfect."

"I'm so happy that you like it. I was *soooo* nervous," Courtney said, hugging him again. "Now, I have an even bigger surprise. I fixed your favorite. I grilled steaks, corn and baked beans. Plus, I have key lime pie. And I picked you up a six pack of Foster's beer. I was hoping we could eat dinner and rent a movie with Cameron."

"All of this for me?" Brett asked as Cameron wiggled out of his arms.

"Of course, it's for you," she said with an innocent twinkle in her eyes.

"I don't know what to say. Thanks," he said, kissing her again. The food wafted to his nose from the kitchen and he heard his stomach growl.

Courtney looked down and ran her hand over his abdomen. "Sounds like we're right on time."

***

The *krump* of mortars and men screaming in agony woke Brett up. Another nightmare. Even after a great evening. Amazing. *When will this ever stop?* he asked himself.

Sweating and panting, he sat up quickly from Courtney's embrace and stared across the dark room at the mirror. He blinked and focused. Wiping a hand over his face, he looked over to make sure he hadn't stirred her from her sleep in his chaos, but Courtney had not moved. She slept with a peaceful smile on her face, snuggled closely beside him.

He leaned down to study her features in the moonlight, amazed at how soft and feminine she was. Her sleek legs were curled into a half-fetal position. Black hair fanned over the pillow. She still smelled of roses and felt like silk. Unable to help himself, he ran a finger over the side of her hip and watched her flinch.

Unable to sleep, he pulled himself out of the bed and made his way down the hall to check on Cameron. He was asleep as well, holding his teddy bear tight.

Brett closed the door behind him and went to the kitchen to eat some of the leftovers from earlier today. The barbeque had been so succulent until he had eaten until he nearly exploded. Making love after that had been a task in itself, and they had both passed out on the bed after and fell into a deep sleep.

He rifled through the refrigerator and pulled out the Tupperware to fix a plate, then went into the den and turned on the television. The news was on. CNN was reporting on the death of several Marines who had been killed earlier in an attack up in the mountains of Afghanistan. Every single time he heard that it sent chills down his spine and boiled his blood with anger.

Stabbing his fork into his food, he grabbed the remote and turned up the volume. As the names of the fallen crossed the screen, he dropped his knife. Shit. He knew those guys. One of them had dated Amy's good friend a few years back. He had even had dinner at one of the guy's house. And now...just like that...they were dead.

The rest of the report fell on deaf ears. Brett sat staring into the television blankly wondering how the families of the men were handling everything right now. He wondered if he still had a number in his cell phone to call and give his condolences. He wondered what the units were doing to counterstrike, and mostly, he wondered if he would make it back from deployment alive.

He still remembered being shot three years ago. He caught the business end of an AK-47 that ripped through his shoulder. Luckily, it was a through and through and no vital organs or tendons where injured. He had still carried a man back, but he died hours later. All he had to show for that was a Purple Heart but he would have happily traded it for Allen's life.

There were so many close calls before and after that until he couldn't even remember them all anymore. He couldn't count the number of firefights or it IED blasts that he had witnessed since the war went down or even explain the sheer frustration of living in a hostile country. Yet, here he was going back.

He prayed to God that he let him come home again this time. The people who were resting upstairs right now had renewed him, given him even more of a purpose than before. It also brought to mind one other important thing.

Considering life happened in a blink of an eye and considering his profession, why in the hell was he dragging his feet with Courtney?

If he died while he was in Afghanistan, he would never be able to come back and do things over. He would never be able to tell her how he truly felt. And he'd never be able to say that he had given her everything. The thought bothered him more than bullets, war or even death.

***

It was Labor Day weekend, and Brett had a 96-hour holiday to enjoy with his family with no interruptions and full pay. He had been waiting for a mini-vacation away from the pains of his job to just be with his family. And now it was finally here.

Marines lived for their vacation days when they didn't have to crawl out of bed before sunrise and work until sunset. The idea of lying in bed on Monday watching television and eating breakfast sounded better than a promotion right now.

Mrs. Lawless had actually asked for Cameron until tomorrow, which meant that he and Courtney had a free day. He still wasn't sure how he felt about Cameron being around Colonel Lawless for an entire day, but Mrs. Lawless had assured him that everything would be just fine.

He liked her a lot. It was their first meeting and the moment he saw her, he knew that she was one of those high society women with tons of class and education. Still, she was down to earth and loving and had greeted him with a warm hug instead of a handshake.

Her eyes had really lit up when she saw Cameron. He ran to her with arms wide opened and called her Grandma Lawless. Brett couldn't deny he was proud, standing in the restaurant with two of the most beautiful women in Jacksonville and flooded with attention.

"What's this big surprise you have for me?" Brett asked Courtney after they dropped Cameron off with her mother.

Courtney gave a big smile but kept her eyes on the road. "I've been dying to tell you for almost two months now," she giggled.

"So tell me already," he said, pinching her side. Leaning in, he kissed her cheek.

"Okay. Okay. Who is your favorite band?"

"Of all time?" he asked with a frown. He sat back in his seat and tried to think.

"No, right now. Who is your favorite band?"

"Um... Kung-Foo Fighters," he answered, scratching the back of his head.

"That's what I thought. And guess who's playing tonight in Wilmington?"

Brett cracked a smile. "Kung-Foo Fighters?"

"That's right," she said, turning to him. "And guess who has the best seats in the house." She raised a brow.

"We do?" Brett asked surprised. "How in the *hell* did you pull this off?"

"Well, sometimes it pays to be the daughter of a colonel," Courtney said, raising her brow.

***

The Blues Bar was packed to capacity with Marines, sailors and women. Waitresses moved quickly through the crowd taking orders. The dance floor was covered with couples clinging to each other, kissing and laughing. Some had gathered over by the pool tables on the second floor to play, while others watched the opening act and slammed down beers. There wasn't an empty space in the entire facility or one person drawing a sober breath.

Brett had not been out in such a large crowd since the last time he came home from Afghanistan. Automatically, he was on guard. Drunk people bothered him. His large hand rested squarely around Courtney's shoulders as she led him through the crowd to the VIP area. Scanning the room, he couldn't help but assess possible threats and look for exits. The loud music, flashing lights and overall chaos made him crazy inside.

What did I get myself into? he asked himself as Courtney looked back and smiled.

"We're right up front!" she shouted and pointed toward the stage. "You won't miss a thing!"

Brett nodded with a smile and shook his head. He hadn't missed a thing anyway. Before they could even get inside, Brett had noticed the stares. Some came because Courtney looked absolutely amazing in her denim jeans and black tank top. Some came because they were an interracial couple. And some were directed right at him from other women who raised their brows or gave suggestive smiles as he passed. Some were from guys who thought that they could take him, but he had already sized them up and kicked their asses in his mind before they could finish looking. Not a single movement was lost on him. Every smile, frown, snicker, whisper, glaring stare and sneeze was noticed.

At the front of the club, a tall, muscular body-guard stood at the red velvet rope with his arms crossed. He looked curiously at Courtney and Brett then picked up his clipboard.

"Name," he said, looking at the white sheet in front of him.

"Black," Courtney said as she rose up on her tiptoes. She looked over at Brett, who didn't crack a smile. Why did weekend tough guys always end up with these jobs? And why did he have to try to tough talk Courtney?

"Okay," the bouncer said, unclasping the rope. "You're in the seat right up front. The names are on the front of the chairs. Enjoy." He looked at Brett as they passed, checking out the Recon tattoo on his arm.

The people on the outside of the rope looked over at them as they entered wondering who they were. To get seats at the front, you had to be very important. And at the moment, Brett felt the part.

They made their way right beside the stage and sat down as the opening band finished up. Brett was highly impressed. He had never been so close during a concert.

Normally, he would get nose bleeds, so far away until he could barely make out the people on the stage. However here, he could practically see what kind of socks the lead singer had on. The idea of how cool this all was started to slowly numb the fact that he was around so many people.

"Thanks for this," he said, leaning in to Courtney.

She crossed her legs and nuzzled her body into his. "You're welcome. You deserve it."

"I need to do something special for you. I mean, you've been amazing." He bit his lip. She looked extra hot tonight under the lights. Her glossy, pouty lips begged to be kissed. Her bright hazel eyes gleamed at him with a trust and hope that he had never experienced before, and her body begged him for other things, thing he would happily oblige her with later.

Lucky to be with her, he wrapped his arm around her and pulled her closer. He wanted everyone to know that she was with him tonight.

"You've done enough, Brett." Courtney felt an indescribable happiness. "This isn't going to be too much for you with the lights and music and everything, is it?"

Brett shook his head and lied. "No. I'm good."

"Great," Courtney said with a giggle.

Again another thoughtful thing from her, he thought to himself. Most women would have never thought about that, but she did. And that was what made her special. There was no way that he would ruin this for her tonight.

He put his reservations aside and committed to being the best date possible.

A blonde, petite waitress in a pair of the shortest shorts he had ever seen came over and took their order then brought them back their drinks, while Courtney pulled out her camera and snapped a few pictures of them. They were so busy laughing and talking to one another and watching everyone around them that they barely noticed the headliner band's entrance on the stage. Then the lights went dark.

The sudden change made Brett tense with alarm, but he tried to hide it from Courtney. Holding her hand, he adjusted his eyes in the darkness. Then suddenly with a large boom from the drummer and guitarist, the lights came on and the Kung-Foo Fighters were right in front of them.

The leader singer of the band screamed out, "Hello Wilmington! Are you ready to rock and roll?"

The entire club erupted all at once, and Brett and Courtney were forced to their feet to cheer on the band. Reaching down beside him, the lead singer gave Brett a high five and began singing. Courtney laughed aloud and nuzzled into his chest.

"This is awesome!" Brett screamed. A bright smile pulled at his mouth.

"I know. I love this band," Courtney screamed back. She snapped another picture of the band and stuck her camera in her back pocket.

What shocked him most was Courtney. He watched her lips in amazement and realized that she knew all of the songs. With her fist pumping in the air and a bright, carefree smile on her face, she forgot about everyone around her and just had a great time. Her enthusiasm was contagious. With one hand around his beer and the other up in the air, he sang along with the band also, jumping in the air with the rest of the crowd.

For a while, fifty miles from the base, in a club with thousands of people, Brett Black was just a guy. He had no worries or concern. He was young, happy and with an amazing girl on a wonderful date that included his favorite band.

What more could he ask for? He had nearly forgotten what such a thing could feel like. Euphoria drowned him. In and out of reality, he moved with the rest of the crowd to the beat as the guitarist laid down a riff that sent chills over his skin.

"This is so fucking awesome!" he screamed to Courtney.

"I know. Right?" she screamed back.

Just then, the lead singer eyed the couple and brought them up on the stage. Brett could barely believe it. Jumping up on the stage, he lifted Courtney up and danced around with the band as they sang their very patriotic rock tune, *Take It to the Limit*.

After they sang on the stage in front of everyone, the lead singer asked Brett name and thanked him for his service. The crowd erupted and fellow Marines screamed out their names and their units. It was a proud moment for Brett and Courtney was right there to share it with him.

***

It was way after midnight by the time that Brett and Courtney made it to the hotel. Courtney had thought of everything. Realizing that they would be drunk off their asses after the show (which they were), she had arranged a room at the Marriott for the night, which was walking distance from the club.

Under a perfect full moon, Brett had carried Courtney on his back to the hotel as they talked and laughed. It seemed they had more in common than he thought. Courtney liked the same music that he did, including Bob Marley and Rage Against the Machine. She also loved to rock out, hated vodka, enjoyed skinny dipping, wondered what her life would be like at fifty, dreamed of being comfortable and had no desire to be rich.

He found her energy relaxing and at the same time revitalizing. She had so much to give the world. And she genuinely loved people. But yet and still, she was okay if not proud of what he had to do in his career.

Getting to their room, he put the key in the door, waited for it to turn green and pushed down on the lever. The door opened and a gush of cold air from the air conditioner met them, cooling their sticky bodies.

"Oh, this feels so good," Courtney said, lying on the bed. "I think I have quite the buzz."

Brett lay on the bed beside her and looked up at the ceiling. "I'm completely fucked up." His voice echoed around the room.

Courtney giggled. "Well, I guess the second part of the night is out then."

Brett's brow rose as he threw his arm over her. "I'm not *that* drunk," he said, pulling her close to him. "Just drunk enough to make you regret taking advantage of me." His eyes locked on to hers.

"Oh, I haven't taken advantage of you yet," Courtney said seductively.

"Cort, no one has ever done anything this nice for me before. Thank you."

"You're welcome." She put her fingers on his lips and traced the curves in their fullness.

"Do you know how much I love you?" he asked seriously. He swallowed hard and pulled her on top of him. He wanted her to see his face and hear his words to know how true they were.

She straddled him slowly and leaned down where their bodies touched. "Yes, I think that I know now."

Brett's voice was low and gruff. "It's horrible to say but the best thing that ever happened to me was that plane crashing. I would still be trying to work things out in a relationship that should have never been in the first place. But you saved me."

Courtney had a twinkle in her eye. "You saved me right back, Brett Black."

Brett shook his head. "No, you're so strong. You would have been alright with or without me. But Cameron and I were lost. We didn't know what to do." He clenched her waist. The combination of alcohol and love overwhelmed him. "You know, when my mom died, I felt like a hole burned deep down in my soul. We were really close. She was always doting on me, proud of me, proud of everything that I did. No one had ever treated me like that, and after she was gone, I just figured that I'd never experience that again. Amy was *not* a nurturer. She was always on the war path, never happy with a damned thing that I did. Even when I was given the Purple Heart, the only thing we did to celebrate was go to the Golden Coral on military discount day." He chuckled. "But a man needs to feel special, Cort. He needs to know that there is someone at home waiting for him, who loves him and thinks that he's special."

"Well, you know that I do."

"Oh, I know. I'm not sure what I've done to deserve it, but I have to tell you that I'm sure damned glad to have you in my life." He ran his hand over her face and moved her hair from her eyes. "This isn't the booze talking either."

Courtney shook her head and spoke softly. "No, it isn't the booze." She smiled. "You make me feel special, Brett. All I've ever wanted in this life was to be needed. And you and Cameron make me feel like I'm a part of something special."

His heart squeezed tight. "Don't ever leave me, okay. I know that at times it's difficult being with someone who is always gone, but I promise you that I'll always come back. I have something to come back to now, and there is nothing out there that is going to keep me from you."

Tears ran down Courtney's face. "Why would I ever leave you? You're the best man I know...*except daddy*."

Brett laughed. He loved that she was daddy's girl even though he was certain her father wanted to kill him. "Yeah, well, Old Man Lawless is a hell of a man. So, I better shape up, if I'm going to follow his footsteps."

"You're doing just great now. I always thought that you Recon boys were hard to the bone. But to see how you take care of your son, how you love him, how you love me...it makes me think that maybe you boys have the biggest hearts. You're always giving, sacrificing and you never ask for anything in return."

"I have one request," he said, running his finger down her neck. He looked up at her under lusty eyes.

"Just one?" she asked, biting her lip. "You mean to tell me with all that muscle you can only do it once?" Her eyes had a glint of mischief in them.

"Is that a challenge?" he asked in a husky voice, rolling her over on the bed. In between her legs now, he pulled off his shirt to reveal a perfect muscular frame. "Now, you're in trouble."

Courtney put her foot up on his chest and gave a lazy smile. "No, I think it's quite the opposite."

Sex with Courtney was different than with other women. He enjoyed her muscular, slim frame, her sexy smile, her fragrant skin, but he also enjoyed how she gave herself to him in every way.

When he needed it rough and hard, she pushed her body physically to the breaking point. When he wanted her slow and easy, she moved with his body in a synchronic grace that made him feel like he was floating. But no matter how they made love, it was always beautiful, never demeaning.

He never wanted her to feel cheap or unappreciated. He would never ask her to do anything that went against her morals. Even though they were not married, he regarded her body, mind and spirit as a pure temple, and he was grateful for her every gift.

Maybe it was the way that she carried herself. Maybe it was the way that she made him feel. Maybe it was just because she was so special. But the thought of her existence was so powerful until he couldn't help but marvel at her.

Easing his jeans down, he watched her match his every move. His pants came off then hers. Teasingly, she pulled off her shirt then her bra. And the way that she ran her hands over her naked skin, over her soft flesh, sent chills down his spine. She was so sensual. So graceful. So feminine. Slipping off her lace panties, she laid back on the bed and rested in the nest of her long, flowing hair. Hazel eyes stared back at him, loving and pure.

She watched his every move, never taking her eyes off of him as he kissed the ball of her foot. Arched into his hand, he cupped her foot to his cheek.

"Did it hurt?" she asked suddenly.

His brows rose. "Did what hurt?" he asked as he kissed her ankle.

"Your wound. The bullet that went through your arm." Her eyes locked on his shoulder, tense and bulging with muscle.

"Yeah, it hurt," he said with a smirk. "It didn't feel good." Looking down at his shoulder, he curled up his lips. "Does it bother you?"

"No," she said, reaching out for him. "It's a turn on. It reminds me of how strong you are."

Brett liked that she thought of him in that way. He slid between her legs and kissed her flat stomach. Spearing her navel with his tongue, he looked up at her with is blue, icy eyes. "You make me feel like a man," he confessed.

"And you make me feel like a woman," she smiled. "All woman."

Running his hand down the outer sweep of her thigh, he made his way up to her breasts. He groaned deeply. "I want you so bad." His tongue lapped her nipples.

Courtney closed her eyes and bit her lip. "Take me then. I'm all yours."

Her will to submit only made him harder. He took her hand and placed it on his throbbing penis. "Where do you want me?"

"Inside me," she whispered, rolling her hips as she opened her legs wider. "I want you to fill me to the brim."

Now directly on top of her, he looked into her eyes and ran his hands down her shoulders. She felt like satin as she wrapped her legs around his waist.

"Don't take your eyes off of me," he said as he lifted his hips.

His entry was slow and easy.

She did what he commanded. Even though she wanted to close her eyes and drift off into her dream world, she watched him. His perfect face tensed as he entered her, eliciting another gasp from her pouty lips as he moved.

Her fingers clenched the sheets. Taking all nine inches of his thick sex was not an easy chore. Sucking in a deep breath, she realized that he was not wearing a condom, but she did not want to protest. The feel of his unprotected body inside her was glorious.

Breathing shallow, she pushed into his erection, the tip of him deep inside of her. Hot liquid lapped between them as he moved in and out of her. His large arms covered her from sight as he rested them beside her head. She looked again at the bullet wound in his arm. The thought of him not coming back from Afghanistan caused a strain in her chest.

"Promise me that you'll come back from war," she said with tears in her eyes. The salty tears ran down the sides of her face.

"I promise," he whispered. Bending down to her lips, he kissed her slowly, savoring the taste of her.

He flexed his taut hips as he lifted himself up and pushed down with all his strength into her body. This time she closed her eyes and screamed out.

"Open your eyes," he commanded.

She obeyed astonished at his hypnotizing penetration.

Slowly, he rocked into her body as he killed her with his eyes. Holding on to his wide back, she took his thrusts as they came one after the other. Filling her to the brim, as she requested, he leaned in and kissed her slowly.

"I'm going to make love to you," he said into her mouth, "all night long."

***

Courtney had permanently moved to cloud nine by the next morning. She woke up feeling like a million dollars, wrapped in Brett's embrace, protected from all danger. This was the first time in her entire life that she could articulate what love felt like. Never having this before, she held on tightly to ever moment like it was her last. But to her surprise, when Brett had woken a few minutes later, he too had a look of utter happiness.

He smiled at her as she curled into his body like a cat.

"Did you sleep well?"

"Like a baby," he said, amazed that he didn't have any nightmares.

"So did I," she said with a grin. Looking at her watch, she yawned and stretched out. "I miss Cameron. We had better head back to get him."

"Dinner is at your family's house tonight, right?" he asked, trying to hide his discomfort with seeing her father.

Courtney raised her brow. "Yeah, but I've been giving it some thought, and you don't have to go."

"Yeah right."

"No, I'm serious. I don't want them to – well, not them, daddy – I don't want Daddy and David to meddle in my business anymore. All that matters is us."

He sat up on the pillow and pulled her up on his chest. "Do you mean that?"

"Yes, I do. I don't need their approval and neither do you."

So, now the ball was in Brett's court. That made him feel even more pressure but it also let him know that Courtney was different.

Her brother's words stuck in his head. Regardless of their disapproval of him, what her family wanted most was for her to be treated with respect. Any father or brother would want that. And one day, he would want that for his daughter. And while having children was not even a discussion that they had seriously broached, he knew that one day he would give her his seed.

Kissing her forehead, he sat up and shook his head. He knew what he had to do. If she was willing to put him in front of her entire family then he needed to be her family.

***

Breakfast in bed had led to a quick shower to-gether and then they dressed and hiked back down to the truck. The trip home was slow and relaxed and the conversation had been basically about the night before and how awesome the show had been.

Never in her life had Courtney *not* had to try in a relationship. But with Brett, there was no effort. They shared the same interests and en-joyed sharing their opinions. She wanted to know what was on his mind, what his thoughts were on life, God and politics. She wanted to hear what he wanted out of life. And amazingly, he reciprocated.

He was always grateful for everything that she did for him, and he never had a problem saying it. Plus, he looked at her like she was made of gold, and he made her feel like she was a queen. Every touch was careful, every word appreciative. He had become something important and needed in her life. He was like air, and she craved him all the time.

How she wished that he had not rescinded his proposal now. Sure, she understood why he had done it, and a part of her felt it to be very neces-sary, but there was a new part of her that could not wait for him to ask again. This time, she would say YES, and she would not hesitate, because she was in love with Brett Black. There was no getting around it.

Chapter Fifteen

When they got home the next day, after Courtney left the house to get Cameron, Brett quickly headed to Jacksonville on a mission. Whenever she went to her parents' house, she normally stayed for a while. And considering they were having dinner, he had a little time.

After spending a night alone with her, no kids, no Marine Corps and no barriers, Brett knew that she was the one. He could barely contain himself when they drove home. He wanted to ask her then. *Marry me*, the thought to himself every time that he looked at her.

Sure, Old Man Lawless and his son could potentially be a problem, but Brett didn't see it as a reason to back down anymore. He knew now. There could be nothing to get in the way of him having Courtney for his own.

Impatiently, Joe was waiting for him at the front entrance of the mall with a cigarette hanging out of his mouth and a scowl on his face. The sun beat down in his bald head as he paced back and forth.

Brett had texted him, then called him earlier, begging him to cancel his plans for the afternoon and meet him for something very important.

Being the good friend he was, Joe obliged and skipped out on Judy and kids at the water park.

Brett pulled up to the front of the mall and jumped out of his truck with his shades on and his baseball cap down and ran over to him. "Thanks for coming," he said with a huff.

"You're really going through with this?" Joe asked. He knew what the important business was that Brett had without even asking.

"Yep, I'm ready" Brett said in a low baritone.

"You're glowing," Joe nodded.

"I am?" Brett smiled. "Well, I should be. I just realized that my future wife has been living with me for the last few months. I woke up this morning with a new outlook on life man. I can't explain it, but I feel...amazing."

"It was that good, huh." Joe smirked. "I'm just fucking with, dude. That's good. You deserve it."

"I was hoping you could help me pick out something that is...you know...classy. I've seen the stuff that you buy Judy. It's nice. And I want Cort to really like her ring, considering that she'll have it on for the rest of her life...*if she says yes*."

"Oh Brett, I'm honored," Joe said in a high, mocking soprano. He batted his eyes at his friend and stuck out his butt.

"Can you help me or not, man?" Brett asked nervously. "I'm desperate here. My life is in your hands."

"Yeah. I'll help your love-struck ass," Joe said, flicking his cigarette. "Stop being so melodramatic though. It doesn't fit you."

Brett's shoulders slumped. This business with Courtney had made him a bit soft.

"*But* being in love *does* fit you," Joe said, hitting Brett on the back. "Come on. We'll pick out something that will take her breath away and put you in the poor house."

***

The entire family was at the house when Courtney arrived. A little hung over from the drinking extravaganza the night before, she slipped her shades on as she pulled behind David's BMW and parked.

While the date last night had been the best of her life, she knew what was waiting for her on the other side of the front doors. The truth. She'd finally have to answer some questions about Brett Black to her father, and she was done hiding their relationship.

Plus, she had never been a liar. She would rather people disapprove of the truth than live her life for her lies. It just seemed so wrong and unfair for everyone involved.

At first, she had shied away from the idea. After all, their relationship could have ended uneventfully and been just one more testament to her bad choices in men. But since she had fallen more in love with Brett, even though they had called off their half-ass engagement, she felt it was time to face her father and admit her feelings.

Besides, she wasn't a child anymore. And she didn't owe her father anything. Still, there was a mounting hesitation.

While she had never made her father happy, she always wanted to. And every time that she let him down, it hurt her deep in her heart. Whether it was about her not finishing school at Yale, moving in with a surfer, being robbed of all her money or changing her major *excessively*, she had never gone a year in her adult life without thoroughly disgusting him.

Without asking, she knew that he would be in complete disapproval about Brett. Her father had always hoped that she would graduate from college, get a good job and become an officer's wife. However, every man that he'd ever brought home for her to meet was impeccably flawed.

Often boisterous, snobby and elitist, she had found out in the first private conversation with every suitor that her ideas about life did not sync with theirs. In fact, she had even gotten into a debate that led her to hang up on Captain America, the name she had given the guy that her father had brought to Thanksgiving dinner last year.

Now, she was about to walk into her family's house and tell her father that she had found someone. Only, Brett wasn't wealthy. On top of not graduating from an Ivy League school, he had absolutely no college education, and *he probably never would*. He was a widower and a father to a child that wasn't biologically his.

He was raised on a farm by a poor family and he was die-hard, enlisted Marine. But he treated her like gold and made her feel important, which was more than any of the men that she had ever been with before had done.

"You can do this, Courtney," she said to herself as she stepped out of her truck.

The sun shone down on her, giving her strength as she made her way up the stairs to the house. Turning the knob, she felt butterflies erupt in her stomach and nearly pick her up and lift her inside.

"Hello," she said as she heard Cameron giggle.

"In here," her mother called out.

Taking off her shades, Courtney slowly walked through the house into the sunroom where her mother was sitting with Cameron watching television and cutting coupons.

Mrs. Lawless looked up with a warm smile and put down her paper. "How was your date?" she asked as she motioned with her eyes that her father was in the far corner of the room in his chair.

"It was great," Courtney said, stepping down the steps in the room. Cameron jumped up from his seated position on the floor and ran to her to give her a big hug.

"Where's Daddy?" he asked as she pulled him up in his arms.

"At home," Courtney answered, kissing his cheek. "Did you have fun with Grandma Lawless?"

"She said to just call her grandma," Cameron corrected in a whisper.

"Just *grandma* it is," Courtney said, setting him down. "Boy, you're getting heavy. In just a minute, you'll be picking me up." Turning around finally, she looked over at her father who sat in his favorite chair reading a book. "Hey, daddy."

"Hello, Courtney." He put his book in his lap and pulled at his glasses. With his legs crossed and wearing a pair perfectly starched khakis and a polo, he looked even more formidable than in his uniform. He always had. "I want to talk to you," he said, looking at Cameron. "Alone."

Courtney knew what that meant. She gave her mother a nod and then followed him out of the room to the kitchen, where she sat down at the table with David, who was using his laptop.

"What's up," David said, stuffing a sandwich in his mouth.

"Hey," Courtney said, grabbing a cookie from the plate in the middle of the table.

"I've noticed that you've acquired an entire family since you started working for this Marine," Colonel Lawless said, without beating around the bush. He ran a glass of water in the sink and looked out the window at his backyard.

"Well, I'm not just working for him anymore, Daddy. We're seeing each other." Courtney's voice was calmer than it was when she usually spoke to him. Looking across at her brother, she pulled the cookie from her mouth. "He needs to talk to me alone, David. Take a hike."

"He can stay. His input will be relevant," Colonel Lawless said, turning around. He looked at his daughter with concern. All he had ever wanted for her was the best. Now this? How could he manage to continue covering up her antics?

"What could David possibly add to this conversation?" Courtney asked with a snarl. "All he wants to do is meddle."

"He's his commanding officer," the Colonel answered. "But I'm sure that you already know that."

"Yes, I know it." Courtney sighed. "But why does that matter?"

"Do you think that you're in love? Is that it?" the Colonel asked. He walked over and sat at the head of the table across from both of his children like he had done their entire life.

"I *am* in love," Courtney confirmed. Her eyes were bright with conviction.

"Courtney, he only needs a babysitter. Once he comes back from deployment, he's going to get rid of you," David said in a matter-of-fact tone. "Plus, he could only be doing this to stick it to Dad."

"He didn't even know that I was the daughter of his colonel until after I took the job," Courtney defended. "And after he found out, he wanted to let me go. He didn't want any trouble."

"But he didn't let you go, did he?" the Colonel asked.

"No. I insisted. Plus, he needed me," Courtney answered honestly.

"So you'll admit that this relationship is about convenience," the colonel said flatly.

"It started out as one. We both needed something from each other," Courtney said with her nostrils flaring. "But we fell in love."

"Don't be so naïve," the colonel said, reaching his hand out to touch his daughter. He looked down at her little hand and felt a swell in his heart. She was so beautiful, so precious. All he wanted to do was protect her. "I *love* you. Your brother and mother *love* you. This boy is seeing you because he needs someone to watch his son. He can't deploy if he doesn't. I've read his file. He's going up in the Corps. Having this child now will only slow him down. This is about his career, Courtney. He is using you."

Tears ran down her face. Why couldn't he see what she saw? "No, it's not about his career anymore. He loves me, Daddy. I know it." Her voice cracked.

"Then why hasn't he come over here yet? I've seen Cameron more than I've ever seen him. Why hasn't he come here to introduce himself, to let me know that he loves you? Instead, he keeps you over there like a kept woman. Why would he do that if he wasn't using you?"

Courtney couldn't answer that. She wiped the tears and looked over at her brother, who was moved by her tears but unmoved by the very idea of Brett Black. "I don't know. I'm sure he was afraid of how it would look...just like me."

"You make sacrifices for love. You stick your neck out for the woman that you love. You don't hide behind her skirt," the colonel explained. Reaching for a napkin, he passed it to her. His voice was softer now that he realized that he was getting through to her. Moving a strand of hair from her face, he touched her chin. "I've decided that you can stay here until you finish school, and

I'll even pay your tuition, *if* you let this boy and his son go. Cameron is a good boy. I can see why you fell for them, but I have to think of you now. You're my child."

Courtney was flabbergasted. Her eyes were wild with pain. "No," she said, shaking her head. "No, I love him. And I'm not leaving them."

"Courtney, take this. It's a good offer," David pleaded. "Plus, we deploy in December. Are you going to stop your entire life to raise his kid while he's gone?"

"Yes," Courtney answered. "I love Cameron, and he needs me. Brett needs me. How many times do I have to say it?"

"What about you?" the colonel asked. "What do you need? I never saw you as the barefoot and pregnant type. That is about all he can offer you. And he probably plans to do so without marrying you. He's going to ruin your life."

"It's not like that. We connect on a different level. He makes me happy. He makes me feel important."

The Colonel cringed. "A man shouldn't make you feel important. You should do that on your own."

Pushing away from the table, she stood up and walked over to the counter. Turning away from them, she clasped her shaking hands together. "All I've ever wanted in this world was to make you happy, Daddy. I wanted to live up to the standards that you set out for us. And it was painful when David could always rise to the occasion, and you could always count on me not to." She wiped her face again. "I'm sorry, Daddy. I really am. For all the times that I let you down, I am so very sorry. But I love Brett." She turned around to face him. "And I'm not giving him up."

"That's quite enough, Jeffery," Mrs. Lawless said, stepping quietly into the kitchen. Looking over at her husband, she gave a deathly admonishing look that made him sit up straight in his chair. "And David, who are you to talk about relationships? You've put the Marine Corps first since before your little testicles dropped. I wouldn't be surprised if you didn't get a wife until your father issued you one."

David's eyes narrowed on his sister, who cracked a smile even in her tears.

"There is someone here to see you," Mrs. Lawless said, walking up to her daughter. "He's in living room."

Courtney's eyes grew bright with confusion. "Brett?"

Mrs. Lawless shook her head. "Yes. He called me on my cell and asked for *directions* to our house." She looked over at her husband. "I expect you gentlemen to give them the privacy that they need to talk."

"Yes, ma'am," David answered as he looked over at his father.

The colonel, however, did not speak a word.

***

Sitting alone in the living room on the end of the couch, Brett waited for Courtney. Never in his life had he been so uncomfortable, so nervous. His commanding officer and battalion commander were in the next room, probably tearing his girlfriend a new one, and here he was in the living room, unannounced and unwelcomed. Still, he knew what he was doing was right. And there was an urgency in him that wouldn't let him wait a second longer.

Courtney rounded the corner with red, puffy eyes and went straight to him with open arms. She had never been so happy as to see his face. He stood up to receive her, giving her a big hug. Electricity exploded between the two as they touched. He could feel the need and vulnerability oozing from her as he held her in his tight embrace. It made him want to hold her forever.

"Oh, my God. Are you alright?" he asked, moving her chin up to see her face better. "Baby, what's wrong?"

"I'm fine now," she said, holding him tighter. "What are you doing here?" She tried to muster a smile, even in her sadness. "Did you come to get Cameron?"

"I'm here for you," he said softly. "I need to talk to you about something, and it couldn't wait."

"Okay," Courtney said clueless to his intentions. She only hoped that he did not come here to break up with her. She would never live it down.

Brett took her hand and led her back to the couch. As they sat down, he wiped her face again and smiled. "This isn't about awesome seats to a concert. This isn't about cooking and cleaning or watching my son." He bit his lip and concentrated. There was no way that he was going to mess this up with his fumbling. Taking a deep breath, he shook his head. "You know, the first time that I asked you, I messed it up. That's why I took it back. I knew that you deserved more than that. I don't even know why I came to you like that before. It was stupid. But I'll be damned if I let you slip out of my hands. I've never been happier in my entire life, Cort. And if you give me a chance, you'll never be happier." Pulling the box from his pocket, he got down on one knee in front of her and opened it.

"Will you please marry me?"

The breath leaped from Courtney as she looked at the princess cut diamond in the black box propped up in his hand as an offering. Her eyes gleamed with happiness and relief. The ring was beautiful and she could tell by the cut and clarity that it was expensive, but she would have taken a gold band right now. All she wanted in the world was to be his wife.

"Don't answer that...yet," a voice interrupted from behind them.

They turned to see Colonel Lawless at the door. He had been eavesdropping and seemed not to shy about it. With his hands shoved into his pockets, he stepped into the room. "Hey, it's my house. My rules."

Brett stood up immediately. "Sir," he said, almost locking his feet to attention.

"Daddy..." Courtney pleaded.

The colonel put up his hand to quiet her. "Brett, it seems you've got my only daughter all wrapped up in you, son. And not just you...your son too."

"Yes, sir," Brett answered.

"But as her father, you have to understand my concern. That's why I need you to know - before you finish proposing and she finishes giving you an answer - that regardless of how I have behaved in the past, Courtney means everything to me and this family. She's a special woman, and I don't think that there is anyone in the world like her."

"She means everything to me and my family as well sir," Brett answered seriously. "Permission to speak very frankly sir?"

The colonel smirked. "We're not on the base. Speak as freely and frankly as you need to. Now is the time."

Brett relaxed his shoulders and walked up to the colonel. "I'm not a hopeless romantic. I'm not fool-hearty or desperate. And I'm no user. I've been to war with you, sir, several times. I've put my life on the line for this country and served you well. I know what you're thinking. I'm not good enough for her. And maybe you're right about that. But it doesn't overshadow the fact that I love, and I'll spend the rest of my life proving it. I'll take care of her, make her happy and I'll never leave her."

"You know that's a promise that you can't make in your line of work," the colonel corrected.

"Something will have to take me away, *just like it would have to take you away*, but you'd never willingly go and neither will I." Brett clenched his jaw. "Give me a chance, sir. I love Courtney. I want her to be my wife."

"So I have heard all day," he said, hearing Mrs. Lawless' footsteps behind him. He looked over at his daughter, who sat quietly on the edge of the couch. "She's absolutely amazing, you know. She sees the world not as it is but as it should be. Her heart is made of pure gold, and I don't want it damaged any more than it already has been."

"I understand, sir. And I listened to what Captain Lawless said to me about making her an honest woman, and I'm trying to do that right now...the right way," Brett explained.

Courtney stood up. "Yes, Brett, I'll marry you," she said, unable to wait on her father's blessing.

Brett turned and looked at her, then turned back to Colonel Lawless. "With your permission, sir." He waited.

The colonel couldn't help but crack a smile. "Permission granted," he said, nodding. "You treat her right. As a matter of fact, you treat her better than right, you treat her perfect."

"Yes, sir, I will," Brett said, turning back to Courtney.

She ran quickly up to him and hugged him again before he slipped the ring on her finger. Looking down at it, she wiped the tears from her face and shook her head. "I love you so much." Her eyes found his again before he bent to kiss her lips.

"I love you, too," Brett whispered into her ear. "I always will."

The colonel was moved by the sight and even reminded of when he first fell in love with Mrs. Lawless. He turned to see Diane in the corner with tears in her own eyes as she held on to Cameron. She nodded to him proudly. He smirked to himself, knowing he had done the right thing finally by his daughter. "Well, now that that is done, why don't you two join us for dinner," he said, turning around to give them a moment alone. "Once you're finished kissing and everything that is."

Courtney released her lips from Brett and laughed a little. "Yes, sir."

Epilogue

Christmas had to come early for the Second Reconnaissance Battalion of Camp Lejeune. Two weeks before the rest of the world could celebrate, the Black and Lawless family gathered in front of the overly decorated Christmas tree in the family room of the colonel's house to open gifts and revel in their last holiday before deploying to Afghanistan.

In the spirit of the holiday, a light snow had even come the night before and gave beautiful contrast to the mighty Atlantic Ocean outside of the bay windows.

Courtney and Brett couldn't be happier. While they had married only a week after Brett proposed in a small ceremony at the base church, the two felt that they had already spent a lifetime together. Every single moment that they could steal away, they spent together with Cameron on family outings and quiet getaways. Courtney had even aced this semester's classes and would graduate with honors after she finished the next semester.

David had even found a special someone. After being blasted by his mother about not having a life, he took a page from Courtney's book and decided to incorporate love into his five-year-plan. Captain Kelly Jamison, a beautiful Haitian-American officer from Queens, New York with a degree from MIT had been his choice. Mrs. Lawless had expected nothing less, and Colonel Lawless couldn't be happier. David sat with her now in the corner of the living room, hugged up and drinking eggnog, clueless to the rest of the world.

For the colonel, this would be the last tour on deployment. With his wife's blessing, he had submitted his papers and would be retiring after he returned home, happy to pass on his legacy to David and enjoy being the husband that he'd always wanted to be.

"Alright, alright," Brett said, standing up by the tree. "We have a little announcement to make."

All eyes went to the couple. As they opened their mouth to speak, Cameron jumped in front of them. "Mommy and Daddy are pregnant!" he shouted with a big, happy smile.

The entire room erupted, and Mrs. Lawless eyes grew bright with excitement. In seconds, she already had plans for decorating the baby room and planning the shower.

"Yes," Courtney said, kissing Brett on the cheek. "We're pregnant. We've known for a while, but we wanted to wait until Christmas. It's our little gift to you."

Mrs. Lawless was the first to speak. "I hope it's a girl," she said, going to her daughter to give her a hug.

"I hope it's a Marine," the colonel said, shaking Brett's hand. "Congrats."

"Thanks," Brett said proudly. He took a deep sigh and smiled at Courtney. "One thing is for sure. The baby is going to have a great mom."

The End

Trivi's Charities of Choice

There are so many worthy charities that need your help. Please consider making a contribution to the following charities to help military men and women and their families in their time of need.

Semper Fi Fund
http://semperfifund.org/
Wounded Warrior Center · Bldg H49 ·
Camp Pendleton, CA 92055
Phone: 760-207-0887
or 760-725-3680
Fax: 760-725-3685

Soldier's Angels
http://www.soldiersangels.org/
1792 E Washington Blvd
Pasadena, CA 91104

Wounded Warrior Project
http://www.woundedwarriorproject.org/
4899 Belfort Road, Suite 300
Jacksonville FL, 32256
Telephone: 877.832.6997
Fax: 904.296.7347

Whether time or money, consider giving back to the people who have already given so much.

STAY IN TOUCH

Official Author Website
www.latrivianelson.info

Email Latrivia Today
Latrivia@LatriviaNelson.com

Follow Latrivia on Twitter
www.twitter.com/Latrivia

Blog With Other Lonely Heart Fans
www.thelonelyheartseries.wordpress.com

"Like" The Lonely Heart Series
www.facebook.com/thelonelyheartseries

Become Friends on Facebook
www.**facebook**.com/**latrivia.nelson**

Visit Latrivia's YouTube Channel
www.youtube.com/Latrivia2009

THE UGLY GIRLFRIEND

LaToya Jenkins is the quintessential woman: smart, successful, grounded and determined. She only has one problem socially - she's overweight. As the "big one" of her girlfriends, she often faces rejection from the men of their social circle because of her size and/or her dark skin. And due to a painful past relationship, she gives up on love completely until, she takes on Mitchell "Mitch" O'Keefe as a new client.

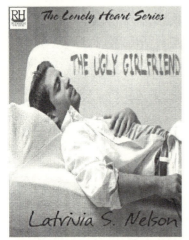

The Irish born architect needs a professional cleaning service to help him literally clean up his life after a nasty divorce, but he winds up finding a true friend in LaToya, the owner of It's An Honor Cleaning Service.

While LaToya is handi-capped emotionally by her baggage, Mitch thinks she's the strongest woman he's ever seen and a breath of fresh air in his hectic life. His only goal is to prove to her that his interest in her is more than lust sparked by curiosity.

Read the story of two beautiful people in totally opposite ways who help each other see that beauty is not skin deep but soul deep in the first book of Latrivia S. Nelson's Lonely Heart Series, The Ugly Girlfriend.

First Book In Lonely Heart Series
ISBN: 978-0-9832186-4-7
Retail Price: $9.99

FINDING OPA!

What does the Greek word Opa mean? According to some it is a word or pronouncement of celebration; the celebration of life itself. It is another way of expressing joy and gratitude to God, life, and others, for bringing one into the state of ultimate wisdom.

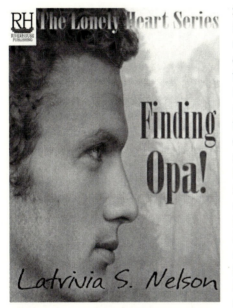

Stacey Lane Bryant has three rules. She doesn't drive; she doesn't travel; and she most definitely will not date. From the outside, this odd-ball, thirties-something, single black woman is simply a creature of habit who has been beaten down by the tragedies of life. However those on the inside know that she's the widow of esteemed astrophysicist Drew Bryant, a highly sought after best-selling romance author and a devoted cat lover. The rules are simply designed to keep her safe and keep her sane.

However, someone didn't tell the Greek bombshell, Dr. Hunter Fourakis, that rules weren't meant to be broken. While at his favorite pub, he eyes Stacey and instantly falls under her spell. Only, his rusty moves don't get him far with the brilliant introvert, who quickly leaves just to get out of his grasp.

What is meant to be will be, and the two run into each other in another chance encounter. This time Hunter is able to convince Stacey not only to go out on a spur-of-the-moment date with him but also to consider an unorthodox proposal that would benefit them both.

Hunter's late wife was killed while serving in Iraq, and he mourns every year for two months and three days. The mourning period is usually miserable for Hunter, but this time, he wants to celebrate life. Stacey's second romance novel is due to her agent in two months but is totally lacking motivation or passion, because she hasn't gotten over her late husband. Considering that they both need someone for a short period of time to fulfill very specific needs, they agree to be each other's help mate temporarily. Only as deprived widows, pressured professionals and lonely hearts, they find that while deadlines pass and mourning time ends, love lasts forever.

Read this romantic tale about two people who fight through tragic personal loss, family prejudices and age-old traditions to find good old fashion love in the second book of the Lonely Hearts Series, Finding Opa!

The Lonely Heart Series
Book Two
ISBN: 978-0-983-28647-9
$8.99

Dmitry's Closet

From author Latrivia S. Nelson, author of the epic romance Ivy's Twisted Vine, comes a story about Memphis, TN, a deadly faction of the Russian mafia and an innocent woman who dismantles an empire.

Orphaned virgin Royal Stone is looking for employment in one of the country's toughest recessions. What she finds is the seven-foot, blonde millionaire Dmitry Medlov, who offers her a job as the manager of his new boutique, Dmitry's Closet. After she accepts his job offer, she soon accepts his gifts, his bed and his lifestyle. What she does not know is that her knight in shining armor is also the head of the Medlov Organized Crime Family, a faction of the elite Russian mafia organization, Vory v Zakone.

Falling in love with the clueless Royal makes Dmitry want to break his coveted code, leave his self-made empire and start a life far away from the perils of the Thieves-in-Law. Only, his brother, Ivan, comes to the Memphis from New York City bent on a murderous revenge.

With the FBI and Memphis Police Department working hard to build a case against Dmitry and his
brother trying to kill him, he is forced to tell Royal of
his true identity, but Royal also is keeping a secret -
one that changes everything.

Who will win? Who will lose? Who will die? Watch all
the skeletons as they tumble out of the urban
literature sensation Dmitry's Closet.

Warning: This book contains graphic language, sex,
and various forms of violence. However, it will also
melt your heart!

The Medlov Crime Family Series
Book One
Available in paperback and e-book format
ISBN: 978-1-6165874-5-1
Retail Price:$12.99

Dmitry's Royal Flush: Rise of the Queen

From the popular multicultural author, Latrivia S. Nelson, comes the highly anticipated second installment of the Medlov Crime Family Series, Dmitry's Royal Flush: Rise of the Queen.

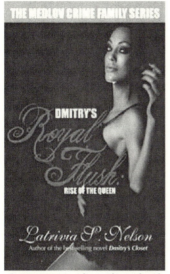

For Dmitry and Royal Medlov, money doesn't equal happiness. Forced to leave Memphis, TN and flee to Prague after a brutal mafia war, the couple nestled into the countryside to raise their daughter, Anya, and lead a safe, quiet life. But when Dmitry's son, Anatoly, shows up with an offer he can't refuse, Dmitry is forced to go back to the life he left as boss of the most feared criminal organization in world. Consequently, the deal could not only destroy the Medlov Crime Family but also Dmitry and Royal.

Royal hasn't been the same since she was attacked three years ago. Where she used to be a sweet, innocent girl, she's now the jaded, bitter mistress of the Medlov Chateau. However, a reality check is in store for the pre-Madonna when Anya's new teacher shows up with her sights set on stealing Dmitry, and

Ivan's old ally shows up with his sights on killing him. Can Royal save them all? Will she?

With a family in such turmoil, the only way to survive is to stick together. Read the gripping tale of a marriage strong enough to stand the test of time as Dmitry realizes that he has the best cards in the house as long as he has a Royal Flush.

The Medlov Crime Family Series
Book Two
Available in paperback and e-book format
ISBN: 978-0-5780601-1-8
Retail Price: $13.99

Anatoly Medlov: Complete Reign

From the bestselling series, the Medlov Crime Family, comes the highly-anticipated story about America's favorite bad boy...

Anatoly Medlov is the youngest crime boss in the Medlov Organized Crime Family's history. Now, he has to prove himself to a council who thinks his legacy has not been well-earned, amidst a grueling investigation by Lt. Nicola Agosto of the Memphis Police Department and during plot to destroy him by his ex-lover, Victoria. In his loneliness, the only one he can confide in is the shop girl, Renee, an old friend who knows more than anyone about his personal journey. However, his friendship soon turns to love for a woman he knows that he cannot have because of the feared code his is bound to by the Vory v Zakone.

When his estranged mother dies suddenly, Anatoly flies to Russia to pay his last respects and discovers a jolting secret. The late Ivan Medlov's own brutal legacy still lives through his son, Gabriel, and his New York crime family. Anatoly's father and former Czar of the underworld, Dmitry, sees this as an opportunity to unite the two major families and blesses both men. However, Anatoly sees Gabriel as a threat to his empire and competition for the affection of his father. Will cousins kill because of the sins of their fathers?

Gabriel Medlov has always resented his existence. Now as an undercover DEA agent, he plans destroy the Medlov Crime Family once and for all. Only in order to get close enough to destroy the organization, he must also get close enough to love his estranged family. Will blood prove thicker than water or will one man's revenge end the Family for good?

Follow the story of one young man who fights to be king in a room full of royalty and suffers the pain of his position in the romantic suspense guaranteed to make you want more.

The Medlov Crime Family Series
Book Three
Available in paperback and e-book format
ISBN: 978-0-9832186-1-6
Retail Price: $14.99

Upcoming Books

The Lonely Heart Series:
Gracie's Dirty Little Secret
Taming the Rock Star
Unleashing the Dawg
The Pitcher's Last Curve Ball
The Tragic Bigamist
The Credit Repairman

The Medlov Series:
Saving Anya

The Chronicles of Young Dmitry Medlov:
Volume 4-8

The Agosto Series:
The World In Reverse

The Married But Lonely Series:
Forgive Me
Sexting After Dark

Paranormal Books
Funny Fixations
The Guitarist
The Pain of Dawn

The Nine Lives of Kat Steele:
Volumes 1-9

Books will be released during 2011 & 2012, but dates are tentative so please visit website for updates.

About the Author

In the last three years, bestselling author Latrivia S. Nelson has published ten novels including the largest interracial romance novel in the genre to date, *Ivy's Twisted Vine* (2010), The Medlov Crime Family Series and The Lonely Heart Series. She is also the President and CEO of RiverHouse Publishing, LLC, the wife of retired United States Marine Adam Nelson, the mother of two beautiful, rambunctious children and working diligently on her Ph.D.

When she's not busy writing novels, doing homework or running a publishing company, Nelson spends her time at princess tea parties with her daughter, Tierra, or being saved by her super hero son, Jordan, during playtime, cooking great meals for the family and watching the sunset with her best friend and real-life super hero, Adam.

Attention Future Romance Authors:

Do you have a romance novel or short story that you want to share with the world? Is it edgy? Is it romantic? Is it erotic? Is it unpublished?

Latrivia S. Nelson and RiverHouse Publishing are going to launch a **e-book only imprint** in the Summer of 2012, Love Only.

We will begin accepting submission in January 2012 and will announce the authors in April of 2012. For more information, please contact Latrivia S. Nelson via email at Lnelson@RiverHousePublishingLLC.com.

The Home of Bold Authors with Bold Statements.
www.riverhousepublishingllc.com

RiverHouse
PUBLISHING